Wolf

Wolf

Douglas
A. Martin

Nightboat Books
New York

ISBN: 978-1-64362-022-0

Cover Design by Brian Hochberger
Cover Art by Nick Mauss, *Untitled*, glazed earthenware, 2016,
    courtesy the artist and 303 Gallery
Design and typesetting by HR Hegnauer
Text set in Sabon and Helvetica Neue

Cataloging-in-publication data is available from the Library of Congress

Nightboat Books
New York
www.nightboat.org

Lyric is my medium, not chronicle.

J. M. Coetzee, *In the Heart of the Country*

As if one alone can build a nest.

J. M. Barrie, *The Little White Bird*

PART ONE

1.

They would come forward later. There would be witnesses from around the trailer. Not everyone who went in there wanted it. Others came over, too. But this was the youngest supposedly. It had never before gotten to this point.

There's crying in some of the places before, before he was not going to be doing that anymore. In place after place, the hands curled up tightly into fists, the face and arms, body purpled, eyes went all red blurring in falling, arms balled up swung raw, and like little toothpicks legs kicked out. Sometimes, even when it might be his chance, the boy cries. At that age it was hard to see one day forward into the next, why the boy would not stop crying how he wants to go back, crying being told repeatedly how if he doesn't learn how to keep calm, it will be forever before he gets to see anyone again ever. Doesn't matter how he had to try to understand there were things he needed. Who is left could not possibly ever, adequately, provide well enough for them all, the youngest, littlest one with a voice that climbed up into those higher registers where it seemed easiest for him to let it all out, everything put all up there into the end of sound.

"Daddy," he tried to say at first, when he was coming back there. All that has mattered to the youngest of the boys for the longest time is having an arm to put around him. There was a certain excitement at first, when he was being nothing but dependent upon him, the father getting a little less quiet, when he saw what he believed was beginning to happen, more, before the other things that are to get turned over against in sleep. He saw the sacrifices he was making? The voice came out then barely above a whisper. Heard the way he said it?

The father would bend down close to the mouth, ear there for him, when always what was that boy still needing, other voices behind them yelled, wanting someone to get over there now. He was his.

Nobody would be doing the caretaking like he said he was but the father. His father knows, doesn't he, how when a boy gets into too many hands, that was when the boy was bound to be changing. Then what was he doing, not being over there right next to him? All the interfering they try to do he's got to get them away from. Could try keeping him from going off to school even, but trying to teach anything in any spare time, anything the father doesn't already know would be too much for anybody, what with what gets left over after working.

2.

The father couldn't leave him alone in the house too long, only if he was going to be coming back real soon, only then would he ever. Some weekends it was to the stores to buy the food, and the boy was taken along, when one would be closing soon. The father was not the one who would be calling himself free, once away from there, once no more of them. He was not the one, driving off in the loud rusting car. Some of them might see it that way, but the father had not gone.

During the week, he would be working and then some weekends. Some of those he would try to rest. When all of the possible causes have to be isolated, neighbors say what a hard worker he was. He is seen out in the yard once, nailing around a window, trying to do something with the place, he said, thinking how he might make it look better. That was not something that happened easily. It was not like every house around there can end up looking like ones on improvement shows. It was not like everybody in the end could end up there living like that.

His youngest wanders off, when not turned down the right aisle quickly enough, dragging around the corners, distracted sometimes in thinking what might happen if he got lost too long in going the wrong way, if he got left there for good by the father another place he might go off from, leave them forever, there in front of one families better off than theirs gave away what they had they were not ever going to really use, places that sometimes gave things for free, if you just asked. There in the front of one of them hang pictures like ones also seen at a flea market, someone looking for one boy gone missing or another.

Some boys give little salutes. That was not the kind of boy he was ever going to be like. Whatever you say sir. Some think they are being cute. Some click together black shoe heels, saying aye, aye, for Sunday school.

What was she doing? Everyone still had to have a mother. The ladies in one store wanted to know where she might be, what they are there that day to buy. Nobody heard right then what was said. It was no good talking. The answer was whining, and maybe he would not want him anymore. The father needed to watch out for him better, before someone else came along to help a boy knock it off. If trying to say anything else, the boy would not finish it. When one is answered, that is what made need fade. Outside in the parking lot wrappers blew around bags of food, skittered cups. Candy went flying when slaps were made. That is how politeness got trained into some. Complying becomes an afterthought. So fast a mouth closes lips practically go all white.

3.

Those neighbors say things, the father knew, how the honoring is to be done unreservedly. A boy needs to go to places like church, still. One of the neighbors herself has a boy, trying to say how she knows how it is, trying to find a way to say she knows how hard it can be, being left all alone there with one. Another woman next door offers to take the boy sometime if he would like? She knows how hard it is to try to keep doing right by them. Or another brings over during the day just a snack for him, offers other times leftovers from a meal already prepared.

They thought they were being well meaning. But they should have known how something was going to happen, when after awhile no one ever gets invited over again inside. Those two would stay together as well as they could in that place they had to be sure never to ruin.

The carpet running throughout it already is all ready for them, no real reflection, as it would be hard to keep clean, when it was only him working so hard every day, just the father, just the one boy? The landlord knows only a little about the man he is renting the small place to, where the father would live last with the youngest boy and another boy that comes back, just for a little while. It was all prepared, knowing what they were bound to want to do, things like eating in there in the living room, while TV played the nights of the week for watching it, and that the only one from anyone they were ever getting, so better be careful with it.

Who's mother was a TV.

Most of the time, nobody was coming over there, at all. No girlfriends, as far as the neighbors could tell, never seeing any kind of a woman over there who might have been one, another offered.

4.

Sometimes one or two men had come over to see the father. There they talked in the living room, boy listening to voices getting turned up. Sometimes the one you were with, they couldn't give you those things you needed. They said things like betting he wished he'd never laid eyes on anyone like the one who had them all, before moving on. It means how the parents weren't married, when they had him, when someone calls the boy a bastard.

Some nights it sounded like shoes going through the house, when it was time for getting into bed, time for school the next day, bottoms of the father's boots with circles the best kind for working, doing what has to be done off there, the father saying like he liked it how others didn't last so long. The refrigerator would open sound, lines grown out light white on cool air before sucked back in. Sounds like someone looking for something, nights when the boy is supposed to be off in bed already, sounds coming through the house, sometimes the TV turned on up but low when someone can't sleep.

Just the t-shirt pulled up under the arms, caught in the light too, sometimes what was underneath seen, colors that thin fade before cut to another, further screen. He shifts around in his work shirt, moves around in his chair, before like out over the skin light floats over him.

He is sleeping there next to the small living room, there where no one for better or for worse hears, this young boy just one of many, and a woman with red lips makes saying something, here skin like another gradient on the screen, noise sliding up over stitching on a pocket, saying a name pumped out onto sound air.

5.

He knew the reason why those parents of his had never been married? Father was already married, once. It happened back when he was even younger. Divorce hadn't seemed so important then, when it was someone they would never be seeing anymore, somebody he was sure no trouble would be coming from, not like the mother who went off and had all those boys.

When it was still a time to believe whatever the father had to say, when he was being a good one, he sat the boy down in the chair, then he carried him over to the couch. Stay there. Whatever they were having for dinner was in the freezer in boxes and from sealed cans because when working all day, and most nights even, things just needing to be heated up would last longer, being careful how much was eaten each day, and he can learn how what he says goes where.

When someone else doesn't hear anymore whatever needs answering, just a boy calling out when he wants to see how if called someone might come, who then knows how to make everything better? They loved each other, must have at some point, but that was not something to say.

The boy with a voice that before too long became embarrassing. The boy had other brothers that had been sent to nicer places, before one of his brothers is back there. No imagining it getting any easier, even when it was said repeatedly to the youngest boy how if he didn't stop, it would be back the way before. Was that what he wanted?

No matter what one started yelling, young and tawny one bawling going to have to see, that's what he wanted? The problem was seeing what all was to be gotten out of the setups of new situations, hoped that the boy was going to grow out of that, hand there on the hip. It was because the boy was so young, someone overseeing cases tried to explain. He couldn't understand, how no one was ever going to want him again. No one was going to put up with this way he was all the time acting. What the boy had best learn was how to keep quiet. It had gone on until finally, an arm taken up to pick him up, a big hand that wrapped around swallowing.

Sometimes it would not matter if you ever did try to scream, when you wanted help or anything else. First the one boy and then the other were supposed to stay back there in that bed, stay in that part of the house alone, while the father was trying to get away from any of his feelings forming.

Some things a boy needed to understand better. Boys, everyone knows, there was a way for them to be raised. In those most right of ways, see.

6.

The boy still wanted his father's hand to hold, something out of which he would have to learn to grow. They said it was that way, sometimes, maybe when he was just younger. The boy called out in the nights when it was getting quieter, and then the father would be there, checking up to see what was the matter. The boy still would some nights in the beginning be trying to move out quietly back towards the couch, over to where the father was supposed to be sleeping, the chair, his, the boy not yet supposed to understand any all the emotions gotten aroused in situations on TV.

That was when it was just the two of them still, his talking to the TV before starting to move around again in his clothes, the boy standing in the doorway that opened out onto a short hall, the boy not like ones who before going to sleep get suspended, find themselves with someone moving up to their sides of rest, hands held, covers pulled at, being told then what they want to hear. He is still a good father. This boy learns the way for going down in the mind, in these times the ones the father wants to try to keep, when it is just like they are the only ones, and having it be like there is nobody else. Eventually he would be there.

7.

It was when the boy's head begins to get filled up with other ideas. If the father was all right with seeing anybody, one or two relatives in the beginning stop by, to see how they were doing, just to have a look in. If he had to get up early most mornings for work, it was not going to be that night.

They knew in that family how the boy was not something the father was ever going to let go of easily again, not after how he'd gone and gotten him back. Trying to explain how they were all related, other family members come in and out of the house sometimes. Eventually, a boy was going to need other things. Like when was the last time he's had his haircut? Some relatives were by there to give the father a break, if they could, if he'd let them, they said. How about they take him off for a ride in a new car, but he wouldn't ever. They knew how he must want that boy growing up, how he must want him to come turning out?

One comes by saying how they can live with him and a new wife, gotten there, just for a little while even stay over at the house with them. And more relatives, checking up, come by. Just for a bit, they said, to try to talk to him. Then this was the way he was treating them? A nicer place, bound to be better off, think about it. Leave whenever they wanted? The father would try to say how he would get whatever was wanted or needed. He'd be the one. He'd find the way.

8.

In the brown and black roped chair was where he falls asleep, when he gets finally reclining back, there along with all the urgencies, those voices buried in the TV, that work their way down in. Sometimes it only takes a matter of seconds to get more settled, soundly after a father's first shifting, flicking of channels, light lines across face, lower down striped then on the body in the chair. In and out of isolated focus go away hours in the room pulled in mixing with voices trying to go back to sleep. On the blue screen screaming of someone followed before his own dreaming sounded, the father sometimes saying, "Go get back in bed."

Near the foot there was where the father would one day only abide him, the boy there already. Even then closeness depends on what he does. This is if he is being good. Near the end is a chance, when you'll have a bit more what you've always only wanted, even if not until one day it had all been earned finally, living. Then they wouldn't be going out of the house at all, either one of them.

9.

They would say just anything at school, even when those others didn't know what they were talking about, laughing done out loud in versions of sing along, when not more normally like yelling. Others try to get at him, in the things they said, telling jokes like on TV. Out from under bars they chase around, springs squeaking mouths flinging back around, and firing pieces of trash thrown down some more, and tetherball punched. How smart someone was is known by the things they said. They want the boy always to hear what is wrong with him. The names come out loud there, outside where feelings are turned up more, other feelings down around the buildings in brick.

He is turned eleven already, though he might not look it, and then twelve doesn't make much of difference when he is mostly trying to stay out of the way. Before he learned, and before the shelter was closed, the boy dropped down to kick around on the floor then went back to where he belonged. At the shelter he acts like he is not supposed to, in all the new places waiting for care, a last chance, and it happens that hands get even smaller clenched when he goes onto the floor. He is so young is the reason, someone thinking they could keep him, and the boy gone on and on squirming away until he backed up against a corner then wall, knowing the minute he went quiet, someone thinking he knew they could keep him, would be able to have him, it was where he would have to stay, all his movements only to ruin all the places, when he wanted to just go home.

Thinking made a space go smaller. Sometimes the right thing could be found, to make a boy go quiet, but there is so much yelling before.

People who know all things warn repeatedly about it, a boy's never calming down, a boy had to stop, before places get all closed up, and he is back there anyhow with the father. It goes on for so long, when one is never big enough. The boy isn't dumb. The boy calls out, when wanting anything else, when still so small wanting help, and they were all bigger than him. He had to stop it, or he knows where he was going. Was that what he wanted, to go home? Exactly all along he's known around these threats to calm down.

10.

Before the older brother also gets back, the younger spent most of his time aside alone there in a room where some of the men took breaks. Nights working, that was where they would go. It was a drive to get out to buildings where late afternoons and evenings got set down, and the printing the father helped out with for a living done. No matter what, the father would be bringing the boy along, always. He would be waiting for the father to get done with a shift, the next one. The father goes there to help with moving around boxes. After is when the two of them get to get out of there. The boy is seen inside at a table used for other things than work for school, but when he was there like that, nobody was going to be getting hurt. Printed things moved past the windows, and a door. He learned to keep quiet. The men came in, leaned against the counter, and then started laughing about how over on the calendars in the other room there were smiling that way all around women with mouths hung angels, like they were getting ready to softly talk when undressed, say something.

How the boy seemed to them there where the father worked was mostly shy, polite, and saying little to any of them, though they saw him back there, coming by the father's work, customers that dropped off things needing copying.

Please, and pardon, sir were the words to use. Doing what the boy said was homework, when it looked like he was drawing, studying.

More things for the copying came in. The boy went back and forth with his pencil, when more of the men came into the room, back to near where stock was kept, and all the free spots in the space is filled up with metal cabinets, shelves tanned yellow-green. Then the father back there says how it would be just a little longer, little bit, more boxes to carry in.

Watch what he is doing. It gets quieter in there when not back and forth with the same pencil, pressed up against the table and coloring out over the shapes in grain designed underneath, that way they color through scratched. Something else the boy would rather be working on? Some place he'd rather be? Someone says the boy is nice looking. Sometimes another voice sounds like it might care, how he might be, what he gets up to doing back there. Taking a nap?

When the fluorescents don't flash, it is darker, and then.

At work people see him all around him, everything quieting down. Then the chairs in the break room get moved closer together. First wait while the men clean up a mess they've made. Everyone seeing how the boy has learned to stay out of the way, and before they go back home, he could sleep if he liked, before they got all ready for bed, ready for school the next day, his head put down, all right. They were going to have to get him a sleeping bag, so it could be brought to work, too. The father would say later when it was time to go.

When it was just the younger, before the older boy had to return too, the father took off his boots, worn for the next shift. They would have something easy to eat, if they were not already stopped by a place on the way home, where nobody wanted to work. Everybody wanted to eat there, but nobody wanted to work there. That was not a place to end up the rest of your life. News flicks, doesn't seem so important, if no one was paying attention.

11.

The shelter had been her plan and big idea. At least for a little while, she'd tried to say, until something else could be done. Some place to entrust all the boys off to needed to be found, when ends could not be made to meet anymore, no her, no boys.

Once she had started saving what she could, it was when she would go. Everyone had to understand. All these feelings had been there for a while, the two having a hard enough time keeping in any one place, a roof overhead, and everyone clothed. She is probably wearing all white the day when something has to be done. There are other boys for worrying about, too. Someone says it would make the situation better, but hadn't. They were tired of each other, then everyone else in the house, and it can't go on anymore. It is when she had brought them into where it was going to be seen what could be found for them. No need wasting any more time worrying that little head of hair, hers she's given all the boys.

12.

They talk to him on the playground, most days at school trying to
get him to say something, say something else over shoulders calling
out around him. He isn't being realistic, is the boy, when acting
like someone was always trying to hurt him, that way he carries
on there. After school, they are going to ride around in that car
rusting out, lips of another who says things just to be saying them,
anything, get all pink, thick up in the face, and tells another one
another day bets he knows what the father does, always trying to
put it into different words, the same insult. Bet they know what
those two were going to do, when they were not off there at the
school anymore. Turn around, so they can say it to his face, hey.
Go ahead, and hold him down, on the playground, while he is
caught, calling for someone. Another position to try to shield in is
hands up over face, or with your arms up over your head, and like
when even younger, going down inside the self, try to find a way
for getting gone.

Bet how one day it was going to be the garbage truck he was
going to be riding around in soon. Here's something to eat, a
sandwich. Putting it back down in the dirt. Know what is said
about who was responsible for his being there, the only reason why
those boys had ever even been born, all of them? That's how it was,
wasn't it, when coming from a place that goes around picking up
the trash, whatever the father is doing, all day, all night.

Looks like still not enough. He needs. Needs to do something more
to take care of them? Look, no one aspires to what goes around
there, all the possibilities meant to shame. See the clothes? Taunts

come in ways chasing more around, shoving around on stalls of the merry-go-round making it go faster, how old, how old, the next step down going to be found. Where was anyone now, they wanted to know. How about he worked in the kitchen now? Is that what he does? Whatever they could think of to say, everyone playing there but him, probably going to be a janitor someday. Something they said just to say things like he was dead meat. Come over there. Others had quicker ideas. Look at the way he was no matter what they said. Even before he knows what it meant, even then already, they were saying the things, until a friend was found how it was supposed to be bad, those things said behind his back.

13.

The friend's place is inside what was called a mobile home park. It was a big place, for a trailer, with a fence that went around the entire lot, high up over the boy's head. One fence around the trailer itself he had made of wood. Inside the main, there were a few more the friend had built, more things. Just because of where it was didn't mean there couldn't be a lot of nice things. They were inside. It was for his own protection, the friend said.

They go over if the father doesn't have to work a next day, a couple of nights he doesn't. Or sometimes just for a bit after work for dinner. He had been just about the father's best friend, for a time. Long time they'd known each other. The bits of the extended family the father didn't want to see anymore knew all about him. He was someone who in the past had been caught at things, the friend, but it had been a few years since. He made his money through the odd job here and there. Stuff like someone's air-conditioner, fixing those up, when it's got to be gotten somewhere. That is a "mechanic," still, and there were other things he knew how to do, too. Saying how it was never too early to start learning a trade, he'd shown some other boys before around there. He had been a friend of the mother, even before the boys' father so much, her and her brother, when they were all much younger, and she was still someone around in their lives, before nowhere then to be found. They were all friends. When the older gets back, the friend says how it could feel that way for all of them, both the boys.

14.

The first time he had ever been brought over, supposed to be good, the youngest must have been around seven or eight. Then they don't go for some time. It could be almost like a second home, if they liked. It would be a little later, a little older, when he sees how the trailer could truly be.

In the beginning, the father gets the boy a blanket with pictures on it of animals in robed colors faded out. The blanket is brought along with a pillow, when they are going nights they wouldn't be home until very late. The father gets the boy whatever he can, though that would never be a lot. In the beginning, on occasion even a few toys he brought over and a game thing held in hand. He can be left to sleep in a bedroom down at the end of a short paneled hall. It was nice to have somewhere else to go sometimes, wasn't it? When it was just the one, it was how it was.

Boys were there for his showing them how to do it. If a boy could do anything in the world he wanted, whatever, what was it that the boy would want to do? What would he like to do, when he grew up, when he got older? What would it be like when he had to raise a boy himself some day? What was he going to do then?

Here was why the fingers of the father sometimes looked like they had the grease on them. Here was how it looked up under a hood. Just like the father said he did himself, the friend would show he knew some things, things about cars. Probably didn't know how they had used to fix them up together, did he. Did the boy's father tell him that?

One of the first few times he had ever been brought over the boy was asked what kind of a car he liked. He answered with the one he knew easily how to say. Corvette. Some nicer cars were around there. Not like the one they were always coming over in, huh. One day they could try to get that one, that Shadow he was going to one day buy. That friend would show them all some things he knows.

15.

In the living room, they talk of how she was, how she had always said she was going to be the one who left. She stayed close until she found someone else, someone she thought could take better care of her. He wanted to believe he loved her, that was a reason, but not right. It depended who he was talking to, what the father said. Everyone always asked about her first. What she needed another one for was taking better care of her. She felt how with a nicer one, nice house nobody would ever be able to get to her. Some of the boys the two of them had when they weren't married weren't even living with them anymore. Must have thought there was something to be said for never having just one of anything. She needed that time alone, to spend with someone else. She wouldn't even look at him anymore. Someone else might become the father.

Five or six or so years of being happy, sure, but that was not how she was going to end up, coming home, saying she had been out, "working." She was only doing it until she got a little older. She meant that every one of the boys they were going to have to get rid of, not just the worst, not only the ones no good, she needed a break, and it was years then without her, the stretches of her disappearing before he was not even counting. He had to know he was not the only one.

He knew the name of the state where she was, and he said how they might go there someday, but that was something they would never do. She goes away first. They had only lived together until she could get some money together. Still think she was coming back? How well did he think she was doing? How well really, off with that new one she'd got?

They would have at her, the men. The father talking about how they shared the house, but then "priorities" shift. Someone saw to that. There was a question of legal custody, but what else to do with the one? It started going wrong when those boys kept coming. She needed to get away, but she kept having more. Some easier to separate, two of them were twins. She decided how she could leave for good once she got them all taken care of, put into good hands she believed, all together, four, but not all of them with the same father.

16.

The younger boy for his part played quietly later on the couch. A laugh track on one channel goes racing around, flipped a last few things past graphic words traced down deep into the room. He was getting like he sometimes would around the father, almost, but the boy was different. He hadn't forgotten about all those other brothers of his, had he? With all of them being over there, it would get louder. She'd gone off and changed her name why. Tell them, they wanted to know this. What does he think she has been doing off all this time? What does he think she would be saying about him?

She was one of those ones who bent over signs in the sky, up and down along a highway gone where the big trucks drove, bending down up there in a position to give a little extra something to go on, get at, urge. Bet he wished someone like her had never even existed, one of the ones up there with hand held out, even though she was going to one day no longer be something for others to do, finger wet in front of a red mouth, then was, a runaway, one way, for others to have a good time.

17.

From time to time, it was on and off, before it started again regularly that at least once a week they went over. Along the tips of one fence around the trailer at the top it was razor-like, sharp in strands of circled wire. Though it was makeshift, touching it even a bit would hurt, and electrocute anyone trying to climb over it ever the friend said. When the fence was opened at night, lights in the dark open out, sweep around in the part of the yard, if ever anyone tried to come up to knock, if anyone ever came over late at night trying to surprise him. Inside was where the friend had himself all set up.

The camera of a security system he had made himself looked out down around there in the yard, a camera set up so that whatever was going on out there he could see, and to the sides, if anyone tried to get in who hadn't told the friend how they were coming over. Pretty soon a boy wanted to know when he could start smoking. Soon it would be that grinding on about how he didn't have any freedoms, not at home. Then he wasn't remembering how old he was.

Pretty soon a boy wanted to start trying to use the words on the channels that played when they thought he would still be back there in the back there, both thought, where he had gone to sleep. Up there, on the couch, the father says is no place for him. He couldn't sleep there. In the back room is a collection of more cameras, in a smaller room older ones. It is good to know how all these things work, and the friend would show him how to use them. He could have anything in the world, whatever that would be. If he wanted to, and ok, once he had it figured out then how was the boy going to go about the making it happen?

18.

Once the older boy got back home, it would be a new situation for all of them. It was something they were all going to have to try to learn to grow more into, when if it was going to be a special school or nothing for the older boy, he was coming back there to live with them. All wheels around them turned, there to the sides of the car driving forward, the younger and then older to work, going to keep on with lives, a situation they would all have to get used to, wouldn't want him growing up like it, what the father has been working so hard for all along, he said, to have them all back there together again.

19.

Driving along by all the buildings that never got too tall, the father took the boys past all trees getting thinner, into an area where there was never plenty enough of for staying behind, going off down towards around where the highway started. He has been lucky, to have been in their care all that time. The boy must have known they were only doing what was right? One day, he was bound to remember, how good it might have been, something for him to think about. They'd done what any family in their place would have, they said. Should have seen that. Whatever the boy might have needed, they had tried to give him, the very best, when they before had him, everything. They did not have to give him anything more. So little they'd asked of him, they swore, a family who had a life all planned out for him, a life for him he was getting away from.

They would not want him there, even for another month. They were not going to be able to take care of him, even for another minute then. They could be no longer responsible. The boys were not going to keep getting those chances they had been giving him, the older one. It had been the last time, the latest in long line of failed attempts, all those years trying to make a place for him in homes. It never worked out, not for too long, though they kept trying. Six years that is longer than the little brother could even remember. That boy had stopped cooperating in any way. For more than six, seven years, they had tried their very hardest with him. Couldn't say they had not given him everything.

What did he think he was going to do? Whatever he wanted?

All any of the families the older boy had ever been with, all they'd ever asked was so very little of him, all the fosters said, asking him never to lie. If he could not see clearly how much better off with this family who had taken him in he had been, if living with the one is going to make it all harder for all of them, that when he was getting his last chance, there was nothing left to do. So there the brother was, going back to another school, because the father had to figure out what was going to be done, nothing but the house, sending him off back to living like before, if he could not at least do those little things he was supposed to do, little things, they'd tried to do right by him, brother was not going to be one of them, that's not who he was ever going to be, all, with the father principle at another, better high school, wife and children matching. Someone was going to have to make it right again. How were they ever going to be able to do anything with him, keeping on the way he was? They'd tried to help him grow up in a way where he was going to be better off than with what originally starting out he'd been given. If anyone could have accomplished it, that last family believed they would be the ones finally straightening out the older boy and giving him some guidance. He didn't want to make something more important of his life, it seemed.

If he couldn't live within a few guidelines simply set down, few rules established. Going on the way he is, it would be out of their hands completely. He would be left to his real father. They asked him if that's where he wanted to go.

They had first checked about getting the permission for a military school. Rather, if nobody could, the father would take care of him.

They would just give the boy back, hated to do it, but they had done what they guessed they had to, when didn't want to keep punishing him, because that boy couldn't seem to learn, when he wouldn't cooperate, even the slightest. That or nothing, the boy comes back to the house with the father coming to get him, and they would all start trying to be together again. He was just going to have to see how he liked it, if nobody else could deal with him.

20.

The two were being watched, when going down the hall, walls down along there chalked out green color inside a painted thick sounding. The boys had not forgotten about each other, had they? Outside the school, walking close to each other, saying something quick, and whispering, they were that way so couldn't just talk normal like you would. They stopped along each other, watched. Everyone watches them. Parents come by, to pick up others from around in front of the buildings of brick, ones who don't have to ride the bus. It was easy to see how they had to be related, riding home together, once they were side by side.

Ones well meaning said such similar things, how at least now they would have each other, the little brother the kind of boy that was going to be needing someone to take care of him.

One works on one until one is solved, knowing then all along then what one stood in for, variables moved around to balance taken up, in each house, every member of a family had their respective places. The problems should be getting easier, when they were gone through every day. Everyone would end up knowing. Algebra, the younger brother tried to say, whenever the father was home wanting to know what he was working on, once in a while feeling it more strongly about the one boy.

21.

Gone back there to live where he belonged he is being looked at, frames of impressions around forming. Those boys don't know when to laugh, not normally when one would. Everyone else did, at points. How was it meant they look different from everyone else? Anyone could tell. All anyone had to do was look at those two, how well off or not they appear by the way they are dressed. The boys stood out there at school because why? One thing is they wouldn't change clothes often enough. This is true especially in the end. Wearing some days what doesn't fit, wearing spots on them, though they try to hide them. Everyone thought they knew how that family lived, thinking outside that they know what it's like in.

22.

Some days out there at the school, at the very first, a few girls tried to talk to him. What was it like, where he'd been before? Tell them. That last family said things like, "God willing." What the older boy told anyone who tried to talk was how there were pills he was supposed take, because of the way his mind works, the way his attention span went. He doesn't really need them. That's what the older brother tells any of the girls at school when they want to know, talking in small groups outside over near a gum smell everywhere before the bus. It was only so long before the mind began to wander off, other things, doesn't know why, thinking of something else. He wasn't taking them anymore. So nobody has to buy them for him. He has to go back there. He was going to live there for a while with his brother, father, see how he liked that, after he had gone off and done what he had.

At one school he used to go to, he learned how to make a bong he said he would bring one day to show everyone. He had stolen a wallet before, something he had never been caught doing.

They heard how there was something wrong with the whole family. They had told him how there was a system, and that system rewards only if you do what you were supposed to do. So many different sorts of people had tried to get custody of the older one, older by a year. Here he was being given one last chance.

It's only normal, only to be expected, with all the working every now and then you might lose a temper people say. He would do anything for those boys, as anyone would tell you. He had not done anything to them yet. The neighbors don't see any of the lights coming on because he will tell the boys when they can turn on a lamp. A small one is placed down there on the floor. The neighbors don't imagine he ever really hurts those boys, no matter what any of them tries to later say, the boys looked at that way all the eyes going over them.

He doesn't push them into the walls, no. He hasn't, not yet he hasn't.

No table, but three chairs fit into one small room painted the same color green their whole house would be, evened all out, chairs for the boys pushed in against a wall with no windows in it to worry about covering over.

23.

There was nothing too wrong with the father seemed at first, when in the end there was nowhere else for the older to go. Saying how maybe it was only going to be for a little while, his having to go back there. All those legal things around it could be dealt with later. He thought he was going to be able to do just whatever he wanted? Must have forgotten how ones like his father and little brother had to live. Seemed the older had shown himself to be too much, to be letting him stay around any longer, when they were afraid of what he might one day become. Nobody knew who he really was, not all about it. He said he heard them say that, how bad it might get, how it might end up. Those ones who'd been taking care of the boy didn't want him at all it seemed.

He might not look very strong at first, but at the school the older is watched going around the track, one running fast. He might not be as big as some of the others, shirts sleeveless, in their own running shorts, and he is not nearly as tall, but here then was a thing he could do. They hadn't seen yet it all, while they watched after him, what else he had to offer, this one thing they should have seen. One thing was running, when those who were well meaning came by schools to get them to think about their future, ones whose job it is to single out one. How best might you use the strength you had, let them tell you what best might serve you in the long run. He should start picking out something to be done with a life given.

24.

What the boy needed, it's thought, even if he wasn't old enough yet to earn any real money, was something like an after-school job. If he was allowed to keep going on the way he had been, what kind of a life does he imagine he would ever have they want to know? They needed to make it clear, how he had blown it for himself. Something needed to keep him busier with his time. What with the way the older one started going on, how did he think ever he was ever going to be able to get one when he needed one? There were some things one could still do, even at only thirteen. Things mattered. Think he was ever going to be able to get any kind of work going on this way he had been? The boy wanted to grow up they guessed unloading boxes like his father, filling cars, or like selling cigarettes up the street or something worse. What's he have in that bag? They had asked only that his homework be done, and for him to not bring home magazines like the ones he did knowing not belonging there. Grow up to have a life like one hanging around convenience stores. Under the bed was a box filled with magazines. He wouldn't say where or how he has gotten fireworks littered in there too among those, none of those the kinds of things to be having around small children. Must have been from places he was not supposed to even be.

They were a better family, supposedly. If you see the way they lived, that's what they wanted everyone believing, to think only one way about them, to by the way they act judge them nice people who had taken him in. Soon he would get whatever he wanted. Where was he going then, they wanted to know, who was he seeing? He answered only how soon he wouldn't need anyone helping him to buy him anything.

25.

Once he gets back there things start going wrong. Of course there had been some tensions all along, like in any family always, but problems have not started getting so bad really until the older one is back there living too, the friend says later speaking inside the grey suit. The older is the one the father couldn't control so much, not like he thought he could and has been all the time the younger. It was when things started to get out of control then over in the house.

They would pull him back away, if things ever got too bad. He just has to let somebody know. If only he'd wanted to grow up better, he would have done right. They say how they could tell already one day how he was going to end up somewhere in a prison, something worse. No options left. He wasn't cooperating, wasn't listening to anybody, even those there to help, trying to do right by him with their values, trying really hard.

26.

For a few nights, it was still no problem, the one getting excited, when they were all going over there, and the friend was trying still to see if there was anything else that he could get away trying to tell them. What else don't those boys know? He would find some things every boy around their age should read, and the boys might need to be taught a little self-defense, he had told their father already, knowing how they were in some places going to be picked on always. Then they could take up for themselves, if ever there was a time when there was no one else around. There were some things he wanted to show them.

Sometimes the heart beat faster. That should be listened to, when it did that, beating out faster beats. That was it trying to tell something felt that couldn't be said. When it is no one but one other, close like it could be good sometimes, huddling, like when you are in the woods, boys off there among trees, it makes heat keeping warm in a night of nothing.

Pay attention, the friend pressing a hand against him there on the couch, arm on around him the younger one jumping up against leg, stomach, there.

27.

Everyone thought they were so smart, when they kept asking the older boy questions, thought they knew how to take anything coming from him. One day back on the bus he shuts them all up, a bus full of ones who don't like ones like them. If they don't stop, he is going to hurt somebody the brother turns around to yell. To tell them how they better start watching their backs.

Better watch out. They would see all how he means everybody, especially that one there, next to a girl who says things making fun of everything, voices, hair, the number of stripes on their shoes, wrong, wrong number. What is on their shirts?

Snickers, looking down there. Don't believe him? It couldn't be imagined, the thing the boys will go on to do, to actually follow through when it has been just about enough. Stop saying it. They'll do one thing, when keep being pushed, those two there, both of them. The older yells at everyone talking on the bus. Soon enough they'll see. It is just the beginning, talking, and they'll come back for them, see how the two of them were with fists, slaps, nobody back on that bus.

He turns around to say it again, knowing where they could go to live. Know how they were going to get it?

They call his name, before the corner is gotten to, where the bus stops. Someone is always then kicking the back of a seat, bumping legs on purpose, leaning down into a face, but not saying anything, around paper wetted up, yelling, lunch straws, what are they looking at.

28.

Then let them see it, he'll be thinking, a color that gets left pulsing. The tendencies were getting ever more violent that the boy displayed. He knows how to make it turn more before it purples, how to make it more red, wrapping hands around himself like a neck squeezed in a big fist where he could too. What looks like it might be a ring of bruises faded slowly, after he squeezed so hard on himself, does it until he finally couldn't take it anymore, vibrating yellow and violet. Obviously, they'd gotten worried. The older boy had said other things before. Understand, they had their own children, grandchildren even to look out for, better adjusted all, and there's been some concern, the boy becoming in daily life disruptive. If he told them the truth, well then they might have been able to do something.

What has he been thinking? They asked him again, when he said he'd kill himself. Then said other things, like people he was going to do it to, said how he was going to hurt somebody else, if they weren't careful. Let them have the values like the family said. Let them keep those kids of their own, kids grown up already with their own.

Towards the end with that last family, they said they had noticed other unhealthy preoccupations. That family had tried to warn about things like fumes eating at his brain, tried to warn what it was going to do to him. Eventually, it would just kill him. They knew what he was doing with the lighter fluid in the shed.

They told him many times, but caught him in the yard again. Breathing that, he hopes it will make them go away, there with the can, behind the shed of the same wood made to match house. What would be next? This was something boys do for a reason. The boy would be upset, overreacting. It was hard to be watching all the time. They still didn't know what he could at times be possibly thinking. The thing has been warned, and the voice in his head threatens louder. It is not just himself. It is their own blood they have to think of, thinking it is time for him to go somewhere else. Something needed to be done with him, how he was.

29.

Here, the friend would show him. This here was the way you meant want, to show it, the friend asking the boy if the father ever told them how sign language was something else he knew. He held out both of his hands in front of the younger and pulled them towards him, closing around, when doing like so, hands got crossed that way, doing it like that, then it goes towards meaning how you wanted something even more. He thought he could be more in their lives. That's why he told them those things he did.

The more difficult years, the really bad ones, those were going to be up ahead. "Love," that was something to be worked more on, later on. The boy knew he was not allowed, but he felt it there with him, being assured in feeling, wasn't he, being someone who shared it with him. He would tell the youngest when it was time to say anything. This way he knew how to do it.

30.

At first the younger hadn't known how he needed him, friend called
that just like the father called what he was.

31.

They were in reality at that other home just too afraid of him, all along. It was around the time of an incident with a razorblade that he had to go back to the father, the brother thinking how they might like him for the things he could do. He had taken one and sliced through a mattress in the room he had been given to use, started pulling out the insides. He was not going to be one of them, that family that thought they had a whole life planned out for him, whole little one he thought he was getting away from. It must have come from the private bathroom he was not supposed to be in.

They saw him coming out of the backyard, that last family that didn't want to find any matches in his room. He had taken with him up the road one of the new containers from the shed for kerosene, already poured out what all they had stored in there. He knew what he was doing? He filled the can back up with gasoline. He had any idea what would have happened, if someone lit the wrong thing? Kerosene meant to burn more slowly, more controlled, all it would have taken was one little spark, if anyone threw one down a match anywhere close, let one drop, if any landed anywhere near the whole place goes up instantly, the stray fire moves up quickly, lawn first red then blanketed black the house of all new green wood.

He gives no answer when they ask if he knows why he has done this, idea he must have gotten from somewhere. They keep trying to tell him different things for different places. He won't just do those little things he was supposed to do.

32.

It marked for a boy beginning to be who he believed he had always been. How. He was being allowed, encouraged even, even if the words for it at first were hard. They had their own feelings, too, kinds the friend would tell him, tell him what and how, when, telling him who to trust. He had to know if he wasn't confident with what he felt it could be taken away from him, time then to pull away, learning to go down deeper into the self, go like breathing disappearing quiet thoughts apart inside where there no one is to see.

Fist balled then opened, along more signs on the way back to the house, hand curled and then opened back up. See how both of them could start to feel their place over there? The father wouldn't want to hear anymore about that friend, he said, saying how he always only wanted what was best for the boys, telling them what they could say about certain things, coaching them in the future.

During the week, it is coming straight home from school the father wants each afternoon. Everyone sees the boys going home to wait. House door is supposed to be locked, always. The door isn't for anyone else, no one but the father. The boys are to be there, in that place never clean enough. Stove is not to be touched. Nothing to do there but go around in heads and they better not be caught doing anything they were not supposed to be. Wait for the father. Wait for him to get home. As soon as he got his next break was when. It was some hours before a car sounded again, the noise the one they have made because it needed something new. They were supposed to be sleeping, or all he wants to see around them there on the floor is homework. One's mind was already all gone away. It was why he was going to have to keep them separated from each other. When he gets back there, don't think he wouldn't know if there was anything else. He would see it, when he looks in on them, come to see what they were doing back there, the boys pretending to do it, as soon as he got there. They would wait for the sound of a door unlocking when they were back in the one room, getting good and practiced at looking like nothing was happening, trying, afternoons at the end of the season before holidays when it still got hot, all the windows shut. Curtains he wanted closed, too. Around the house outside it looked like any second it was going to start falling in, the house the boys began to dream would not even be standing anymore.

Down through parking lots, before dying run and police make a body in a corner, carry it down, shows with chases before it gets to this point. Another channel, a judge, News. Same hair, different woman, she does something funnier with her mouth. Toothpaste gave the whitest teeth anyone had ever seen, you wouldn't believe. The shows there in these regular places are there to help, supposedly. Someone was being lead away for the way they were being. The chest gets tighter, the younger one there on the floor, no father's feet curling around anymore. Even when the boys were no longer parked there, pictures thrown over in light still licked up the walls.

33.

Light bounced off the side of metal of guns hit, shapes near handcuffs. Repeatedly, they keep asking the same question because they need to know. Anything the boy wanted, while they were there, waiting, ask ones in bright shirts, shirts white and tucked in beneath pulled ties, belts brown roped into pants underneath matching everything. All they need to do is ask, those boys. Nothing they need then, nothing at all?

The two answer with manners on them, no, replied, sir.

Important people to be respected are going to be speaking to them. He couldn't remember whose idea it was. Later, they'd say they were afraid. Later, the younger one in the court will be at the table in the front, holding onto a pencil. Pictures are put down in front of them, in the court, pictures of boys, things on and off. At what point does execution of such thought become plausible? Eyes kept on them. He told them what to do, that man there in the grey suit, the friend in the court?

34.

Judges of them, the jury, they would be trained with separate verdict sheets, working in the absences of any prior justice. The gathered there would be to determine the sources from which crimes had issued. Sitting with each piece, guilt degrees would be based upon how factors were felt to line up. There would be sheets for each boy and another for the friend, each sealed until each one is in.

35.

Before and after they went over to the trailer, before and after school again, the younger brother got out his pages, like he was trying to concentrate, hoping they wouldn't say anything, pretending like he was doing homework again. It gets warped around, holding bits of it up to his chest. The bell would ring to dismiss, and they'd all go for the door, trip to be gotten through without anyone trying to look at him. It is hard separating out all the eyes that go over him, after the teachers have asked again him to change where he is sitting. Even when good sometimes there was moving, everyone watching the way the boys rode the bus home together, the older brother now there beside him. Knew how living got done there in that house they went inside of, and hearing everything being said.

Waiting for a boy to react is why everyone was staring, kept looking at him. He had tried to learn to not look at anyone, tried to learn how to push back down inside him any feelings. The right things, they would never be said, and that was why at school he put down on his desk his head. That was why he was trying to get all up there, next to his own chest, the boy carrying pencils, and in his hand a book, the spiral, things he will say were for school. He'll get it out when they get home, where he'd written by erasing away the colors in spots, on the cover marking out letters, "Private."

36.

When it comes to them going to the court, the younger boy will be given a yellow legal pad to use. One letter to be received by the friend will be passed along, just to see what he might in response say? Only thoughts made them the way they were. Then everyone there was set to make sure how it never got to the friend again.

Putting the things on the page the boy doesn't know even how to spell he tried to keep looking down there, focus like his brother saw him when he was home in the living room, and the father was still trying to talk to them. His words assembled there everyone sees. No need to write everything down, any more. The boy thinks of them so much at points their names run together, running together in words on page, thinking letters, words might still be gotten to him, easy to spell, just one particular example, shown around the court. He wanted it from boys like them, they would say. Is this how he was supposed to be? Proceedings moving beyond the examining of sheets.

37.

When the friend was younger, he couldn't bring any of them back, when still holding down a regular, steady job, before he had even gotten to know at all the father of the boys. He thought no one would see, when he kept keys leaving a shift, keys he could get anytime. It was something to do, to be anyone's friend. If some boy comes by he had somewhere to stay for free, the motel providing a bit of shelter. There were things to drink, if that was what they were looking for, wanting nights come by. They could do whatever they wanted there, just as long as they were quiet about it. He had to keep it not getting too loud. There were things he could get them to eat, other things too in one empty room, nights after some shifts some things to smoke, more coming by, somewhere warmer, other boys who had just to be quiet when let in. All of them in one room not being used, it would be fine, he thought. He was supposed to be working the night of the police getting there, looking around with a number of boys on the bed.

A boy was running away, that's why he's been invited in, that's the story when caught there, though never before does it go as far as it would the last time.

38.

Anytime any of them wanted a new game, he gets it, kept around
the old stuff new stuff too. Anytime the boys came over, there
were videos for them in the back to look at, other games. On one
of them, you ran before anything shot down at you. New playing
was learned, a skill to get through to the end, system kept new.
The friend has a newer computer. Typing in whatever name
brings up everything, to find out about anyone, anything. Over
there were radio scanners, two-ways, shortwaves, from days when
the friend said he was a volunteer fire fighter, on call sometimes,
said sometimes he still was, though never really needed. In the
back part of the trailer was where you could hide, if anyone comes
over, tries to drop by, because the cameras out front don't always
manage to pick up everything clearly, you don't know who's out
there. He has cut down into a part of the floor, for a place where
the carpet goes back up over it, and made a door for crawling
down through underneath. That way you can move around under
it. Nobody will ever know how you are getting out. The room
the friend has begun working on is going to be big enough for all
of them, and there will be the whole setup in the back part, TV,
computer, pallet made there. The boys can take one of the radios
over to their house, if they want, so they can talk back and forth
the nights they aren't coming.

39.

The first time the youngest runs away, he knows where to go, though the friend would have to turn the boy back over soon to the father. He was the one making them always having to go back home, leave from the friend's. He had said how no, they were not going over to the trailer anymore, before being at home with the father had begun feeling like being trapped completely inside.

When the boys aren't off at school where they were supposed to be, he could see how they needed someone like him. Whenever they'd go over, he's asking the boys how it has been that day. He can't seem to keep his hands off the one anyone would see when around there, when doing things like playing a game in front of the TV, played with fists curled tight locked down around intent on completion, a vengeance playing, hands traced out purple wrist flicked gone more red more tired first then image blackened on screen.

With his homework, the boy is supposed to get all the numbers lined up even, nicely spaced. With the homework, he is supposed to try to get all of the letters even, round, to not pick up the pencil until at the very end of the line assigned, cursive connecting across letters legible, his writing a kind of scribbling, veering into the appearance of more frantic at times.

Drawing another letter, the boy would think about how they were going to get away. Give it another year or so, and then it might not be such a big deal, thought at first, the things that shouldn't be, the friend said, when it could happen, a bit more to see.

When he feels it beginning, and when it wouldn't matter. When, the brother was asking. When could they leave? Whenever they might be able to leave, they still wanted the friend waiting there for them, didn't they? Got to get his brother to be patient, just a while longer. So this was the way it was going to have to be if he ever wanted to see him again. So if the boys had any ideas, tell him, tell the friend. Soon things were going to be better, for all of them. Waiting was hard but sometimes you had to wait. He would let the boys know when, how, living with their father, it would only be just a little while longer.

40.

Yes, the man is feeding them then. They were being clothed, sure, but for how much longer? The younger would say he was not going back over to the house, not unless his brother was there, because his promising how he was going to take care of the both of them. So they were going to have to find a neutral spot, a place for the friend to give the boy back.

The friend asked if he could, before he said goodbye, take the boy out from the parking lot where meeting had been arranged, because the boy is hungry, wants to go across the street. Across the asphalt lot, he would watch, even from afar, he would watch. Let him feed him first. He'd get him something to eat, the friend said. He said it would not be too long they'd be over there, if the boys' father would let it.

That boy was going to be getting whatever he wanted.

They could go on ahead.

There is plenty to be gotten inside, while the friend tells the boy how it needs to be still, how it was going to mean being more careful when someone else to think about. When, the brother would keep asking. If either boy wants things to work out, over at the trailer, it is very important for them to keep doing it the way the friend would show them it could be. With their father, do like the friend says. There was just a bit more to see, for when it could happen. Things to be. They need to all be friends. Don't let the brother forget how it goes over at the trailer. Then he would come for the both of them, when it was time. He didn't have to worry about that.

41.

He must be seeing what a nice place it was, where he was before, the older boy trying to come back near there them, where they had a pool even seizing in the light, and over all the sound they had to try to get ahold of him. Just a week or two, it couldn't be more, after the older boy had been given back to his father and tried to run back.

If he told them the truth, well they might be able to do something. He gave them no answer, when they asked him why. Was it something he'd seen that made him start acting the way he was? Trying to calm him down, talking to him, all of the members of the family who were say tell them, exactly, how was he being pushed around? The man was his father. He was trying to say that, but he can't be, the boy said. It just hadn't been long enough. He only needs to see him the way he is, get to know him again, see him the way he was. Reason. Try for a little longer. What didn't they know?

They didn't know the way those boys were being treated. What was he doing? They wanted to know. They needed specifics.

What was he really? Things.

They have a number. They were calling over there to tell him how the boy needed to be picked up. And his brother he tried to say something about. He could not let it go. It started up racing in his mind like back when younger, smaller, left alone with a man they kept trying to say was his father. All those other locations from before in truth with their associations. Better for him to just make up something. Listen to him. He wants them to see how when they were forced with him he was only hurting them. His brother especially. Listen. The little brother doesn't remember. But he knows it already, how much worse it can get, knows what he'll do too first chance, the next chance he gets, as soon as he can he knows what he'll end up doing. He is still going back to him, though.

Next time he tries to come over there, the family has to call the father.

The father doesn't have a phone. Whenever the father needs to make any calls, he does it from the gas station up the street, even though people are always telling him how it was something for their own good, he would get them whatever at the time he could afford to for them.

They push him marching right back out of there that last family that couldn't take it anymore.

There is even a bruise to show for it, outside, the boy claims along with how they were being pushed around by someone always wanting them to call him what he's not. The boy keeps trying to tell them, he's trying to tell them, he only wants them in the one room, won't stop trying to push his brother, pushing them both in there. He knows what that man was going to do, wouldn't stop saying the things he'd do to the both of them locking them in. He wanted them to see how it was already getting rough. How had he gone and gotten out, if it was really like he says? How'd he gone and then gotten back there to them?

42.

It appeared to the police, sometimes, some of those days the boys must be driven. They would have had to have been, some of the distances gone too far for by foot, the police posted out to look for them, and then the father was doing his own looking too, as soon as he could, just as soon as he got out of work.

43.

One time they ran away the father goes over to the trailer, seeing how it is he guesses not where they were, either, though the youngest had been hiding in the back, the friend always telling him when he could come out again. Then the friend calls the boy over to the phone, so he can leave a message there. He is able to be there with him that whole week that the father goes around looking for both boys. Nobody sees inside, how the friend has his arms around the boy, while he talks making the message, standing right there next to the friend but recording so it sounds like, based on what's said, he's off somewhere else, sounds like he left a message for the father from a gas station. The message says how he can stop looking. The boy doesn't say when he is planning on coming home again, but he does say how he is OK.

Guessing what the younger must have been wearing, the father told the officers what to look out for, probably the jacket he never took off, hood the boy tries to hide down inside, jeans sagged below a t-shirt swallowing around him. The younger doesn't wear shorts, not like the older, seen last, that last time he ran out, in basketball shorts, blue with a white trim. Even though close to the end of the season but warm, he was wearing a t-shirt not saying anything.

A car that was a police one flashed, before then came the lights. The police officer notes in report how when the older one is picked up the boy wasn't wearing any socks, and the boy was carrying a lighter.

Smoke?

The older boy shrugged in the back of the car marked. One rule: no smoking in the house. The friend has given the older money for cigarettes, if he wants any. A police office is talking to him in a routine way. He knows better than to fall for that. Doesn't he know what might eventually happen to those boys?

It was before they are in what is on TV called holding. It is called harboring, the way those boys were taken in. Smoke. He had to have known they would be caught. They must have gotten what to say in times like these from somewhere, must've gotten the manners from somewhere else. Just how long does the boy think he could reasonably stay gone? If a boy is only twelve, thirteen even, they can call it kidnapping, as concerns that "friend," so-called. They hope that this is the last time that they would have to intervene. The older shrugs shoulders a little stronger, again. Then he won't be saying anything for a long while. He isn't going to talk anymore, only later to confess how he was hoping it wouldn't end up like it does. That was why he runs.

44.

Whenever they are caught, the boys are going back to the father with a chair full of papers, cup held down with him there in it next to his thin stomach. He moves the warmth out from under his work shirt, front flap opens down to a shirt stretched, some days left on himself still in the house his jacket patterned with brown trees, for going in and out, slipping out of, camouflage that needs washing. He pulls the cup up to the side of the chair, to leave it there. In the chair is where he starts to make those noises in his mouth he made. What stays in the head of the older is the sound not funny, almost like huffing, slacker, wetter, when the tongue moves back behind teeth, gone more deeply inside the body at rest not yet woken up, air inside around stewed. It was never too long before it opens the way silver inside fillings turn up, boots down around feet loosened.

45.

Didn't matter how many times they tried to run away from that man, both boys were going back there to live with him and they knew what to call him.

Some nights in the trailer, the younger will try to sleep up there on the couch, the friend saying to the father tell him, he would wouldn't he, if they need anything? One day, he's going to have to admit it, how he might need a little help with them. Some things were OK to admit, to accept that.

But he got afraid, didn't the father, anytime any feeling like closeness started to happen.

The boys would see each other over there, when managing to stay gone one time for a whole week, before the police come and get involved. It's because there's still the father to worry about, like the friend says. That is why boys always have to end up fleeing.

As far as the Law was concerned, it had only ever been minor things before with the father, a man still pretty young himself, and what happened in the past only happened when there was no helping it. He's been trying to stop himself, a few time drunk driving but had work to get to still. Those few times stopped without a license, one or two times a check bounced, all he could do. Mostly it is perceived outside the house how he is controlling these things, telling the truth, he said, guaranteeing it to the police, all he has been trying to do is find a way for getting all his boys back together, been wanting for some time just a way to start over.

46.

Over one of the weeks for times the younger doesn't know where his brother goes off to, but if they both got back to the trailer, if the friend had both of them there, it would be a way to manage things. If the brother didn't want to come back there, he doesn't have to, but he wanted him to know how it was a place where they could always. They can go separate ways running away, if wanted, still one day meeting up again where everyone knows.

Behind less lone stations, the friend would be there, looking for boys looking for cars or anything. There behind one, the older brother had tried to stay.

Boxes go down on top around there. Walking down the road once, he'd gotten as far the next day as a new town that shows up. Leaves feel when up against the skin soaked. It is back behind one store he just has to get back to, convenience, gas station, back parking lots that give way, back behind some that for bits and stretches of a little woods exist still, thinned along to grow up there subdivisions changing from bad to good neighborhoods quickly. One is set to have a pond inlaid, a man-made scene. The small primitive shelter is rigged there, because if it gets any bigger it would be seen. Quickly too it gets worse.

Other boys looking to try to sleep ran along through new houses being built. Others hide there among timbers before occupied fully. Pulled together are pieces of construction, all the boxes discarded not fully yet used, parts of plastic, and other trash always there back behind one store. Even further along behind one a tarp leans, before further out into *woods* all left traces among what was to come next.

47.

No problem with him, the friend said, if that's what his boys wanted, knows he doesn't like to leave them there all alone in the house. If the boys don't want to ride the bus anymore they were always saying, and if the father has work, the friend can pick them up. One thing he won't have to worry about, and the friend can easily, no problem. There are people, like him, who could always help out with things, if he would just let them. Not a problem.

It would be better if he wasn't always having to take both boys along with him anywhere he might have to go, anytime he is getting up for going, he tries to assure him. Won't it, while hands sweat.

The younger would do like he was told. Get up off the couch. Come back. Get them later, sure. If the boys would rather stay, no problem. First the father thought it might not be. The younger would ask again could they?

One night before it is all over the older boy walks out of the trailer, says how he is fine, and when they asked him where he was going, how he was, going to walk, going for the door, tries to say something about a girl at school, someone he wants to go see.

When he was done, call the friend. He'll come pick him up.

Didn't want him having to walk all those roads all the way back, or that's another way to stay gone from the father for days. Tell the friend where they'll be, wherever either of them wanted him to come get them, call, that's something they could do, and he'd come pick them up soon as he could. He offered, how he would be there waiting.

48.

The father wanted to hurt his brother. How was he hurting him? There's just one answer to everything. He's their father.

Still, the boy couldn't stay there. Sitting back in their own easy chairs members of a family try to say how he has to see. Now why should they believe anything that boy said to them? It was easy to tell when a boy like him was making up a story, because of the way he had of staying a little vague always.

Most every little bit that had ever happened up on or around the couch, that roughness of that fabric touching up on his parts there felt in places like his chair. The first time those two would be able to do whatever they wanted, more things only then, all those things they've been waiting for, one day, until one day, what they need is for it to be a first real time together like it was being pushed down into something that goes on for a long time.

49.

The friend was not the one saying anything about being too young. He was not, he said, putting his arm around, voice like it got all pressed down. Being the way he was he told the younger he doesn't have to be embarrassed. They'd known each other for a long time, right? Anything a boy wanted to say, it was easier, bound to be less embarrassing to the friend than to the father.

Knows about life things.

It'd been a while since over at the friend's so he could relax. When the father had drunk enough, already, if, he's trying not to too much, one, two, just some. He'd ask. They'd see.

50.

Down inside in a space, where one was going to be bound to beg, where they'd be fighting back, trying in a scuffling one night, while others watch shows on still about living how to be better off in the end than this. On and off, clicking, flipping go the TVs back to other channels. Once they got him back outside, could he just walk back down the road some? They had better not see him ever again next door, catching him trying to come back around there, seen lurking, crawling around in bushes near the side of the house, in lights awash, seen trying to get back away before he took off running, once he knows how they can probably see him, way the stomach and the legs make shadows on a wall and he won't stop coming around there. Couldn't the one see how without him they were a family still, who in the kindness of their hearts once had opened wide before to him their door? Who else does he know over there, near the house?

They would call out the doors. He would take off running back away from them all. He knows where he needs to go, where he belongs. When he is running, when the older being threatened, boy being, where does he think it was ever going to be he would be able to go away from himself forever, get away from himself? That boy could barely be held onto when caught, but they will, with his best interests in mind they said they had but had their own. It had not been long, and there he was already, saying how he is looking for some help.

51.

Not that once they weren't going to stay longer. Again asks the boy backing himself up there on the brown couch in the trailer.

It wouldn't look right.

The little brother climbs up closer next to him, brushed on the couch. Way he is moving it means he loves him. The little brother was used to being down there in the middle of them before back when everyone just about fits up onto there the couch, and never any need before to bring a chair in from the kitchen area, the TV within arm's reach. Like he's starting to become a little man.

Thought he was.

The father, helped to settle then in with his drink, pales. Sitting there so all the eyes were on them, talking.

His mouth is held shut places where words rolling over the ears are there from the outside. Grown a little bit, hasn't he, since the last time all of them had been over there, where better TV was.

They would be going over, nights still. Some nights in a row sitting there when the father feels back at home like nothing but a body in a chair, and in the trailer it is getting later, this where the father liked to go, where he did the things he'd once done, a lot more before there were his boys around. Smoking, but not much, gurgled inside glass. They could stay if they liked. He wants to get the father something else to drink. If it were up to the friend, he would never make them leave. TV on over there, so the boys could watch, voices lowered, when they drink sometimes deep into early morning more smoking, the boys can do whatever they need to do for school when they get home. Promise. Sometimes

gets up quickly walking them all out, opening the door to the yard a bit there in front, over where the brown car is pulled up in shadows, some nights mumbling, touching him on the shoulders some without thinking first. Nice to have somewhere else to go, wasn't it? Some nights shoulder, then the next, keep rubbing, if he let him there on the couch say how they could come over anytime they felt like they needed to, whatever reason, they could. Sitting there with him on the couch a feeling inside he should be moving further away from, though closer he got, and it is while they are all there, in front of the TV in this part where the attention begins to shift over around in the room.

He was learning this way he'd be somewhere else. It was like the boy would get sometimes around the father, but different. All those names they'd given him off in other places, all those other ones they called him by, they meant nothing, they didn't have to sound like them, not really, if he didn't want them to, be just the kind they called him by. Not the way they said it about him in any of those other places, those other names. It didn't have to be bad. With the friend, the reason they didn't want to say anything yet about feelings was because few people would understand. Not until someone like the father can get used to it should they even try speaking about it. All that was going to matter one day always was what they felt inside.

52.

Between sessions, there would be recesses. They would need time to think over harder what would have been done. Then get ready to go back into the court. A whole year would pass, before any numbers for them would be decided. Others too then. They were the ones who were going to have to go forward with this.

Listen, while they rise and the play of the court takes its time. With a light on the floor, another steps up to the mark to raise a hand, right one. Put the other one there, and hands down, sitting like told.

Yes sir, as to understanding, what would be going on there. Facts changed, though not completely.

Best not to get too close to them. Best not to imagine being like one of them, having felt what either must have at one time or another. Something to grow out of before too long is the way the little one crossed legs crossed under the table.

53.

One night the friend asked the older boy about school, any girls in his class. He wanted to hear what he would have to say. He could have his own feelings. The father leans laughing, hunching up a bit at the end of the couch, reaching down over towards a beer can there on the carpet, flattened around boots from work still on. Knees spread, he rests it up there against the inside of his thigh, the brother looking, like he tried to focus too at times when the father tries to talk to him. It was how he could be one day, this here learning to be.

It was no more than seven weeks of the older being brought back there to live with them in the house, getting on into the second month, and he knows there was no way he was going to be able to stay there. Some things couldn't be happening anymore. The older knows how he is the one going to have to keep his little brother safer. He knows how it was going to end up happening.

He watches them with whatever is on the TV, the friend trying to make his own place a place for them, the friend comparing, like with others who used to come around. He holds his hands up to him, then to the feet of the boy. Only that much further, before he had caught up with him. Some of his features, they still had some developing ahead of them. At some point, everyone gets at least a little bit taller.

Before too long a voice starts to crack. Some nights it got hard, to tell exactly who words were for, when they talked. How about somebody goes out to get them all something to eat? The radio in the back begins to crack. No problem, whatever they wanted, the friend said.

The friend's hand rests on the back of his head, patting, rub cups along the neck. Make yourself at home, told them, repeatedly. The father got up to go for the trailer's refrigerator. He was there for them. He would be, no matter what, the friend told them.

Putting hands on him around him like that walked them out, when the father has come back from seeing if he could see anything out in the yard, looking for something wrong with both he couldn't find, when trust was being learned, looking up at the sky.

54.

The younger brother pulled at the sides of the couch, then up under his shirt. Once he's taken off the shirt that doesn't fit right, began to feel where he goes, belongs in this place he feels because of the way he is made. He's decided, because of how he is, he knows now. He writes it on pieces of paper, like it was going to happen the way he wants it to. He knows what love looks like. This was how at first it was going to feel, he has to know like the friend said. Nothing was happening, it was not how it looked. Would say it was for school, all those things he was writing, if ever found. It was how he was, before he even ever became such friends with anyone. Love is the reason he is feeling. Nobody knows who he really is, and not about it, he'd say, he writes. Sometimes you meet someone, and that changes a person.

55.

It wasn't happening yet, in the bending down to hold onto him. Just kissing, sitting him on his lap. For a while, counting forward birthdays. The body of the friend is so much bigger sliding under it is like hiding sometimes, the brother with his bending over him, words in a mouth come out all weird wanting over him. The couch in the trailer gets full of a smell, and then they would go back there to where shade of sheets on bed is hard exactly to say, but already the cover is pulled back sometimes, it's not even made up, ready there, waiting for them, that room they go off into when no other people are around, nobody else is close, headboard there against a wall. The friend does it again in front of the brother.

At school the quietness is to be kept, too. "Phasing out," the boy learns. There was a moment everyone wouldn't stop talking about, coming outside before and then on the bus again. Everybody wants to know who has done it, and who has not. They ask everyone around, everyone beginning to try to guess, boys and then girls. Has anyone else? With who, huh?

He should start paying better attention. If the boy doesn't want to be like his father, he needs to get better in math, plug it into the equation. If he paid better attention, then he might do well enough where he'd be moved up to higher classes maybe sooner.

Others around and out of the corner of eyes are seen kissing, kissing around in the parked cars, bus starting to slowly move, and barely able to, for all those cars parked there but then budging out.

56.

The father sometimes not even there. Not every night will they but nights there is nothing else to do. He'll be coming back for them, after leaving them with the friend, when offered. Anything the father needs to do? Tell the friend. If he has to run out for something, or just wants to go for a long drive ever, has some thinking he needs to do, something for a change, leave them a bit, it's fine, use him. He knows how he doesn't like to leave them alone. Just a bit.

Arms and knees support the body, a bounce and even shadows when the brother sees positioning, before a weight comes down. One night he watched the tint of a kiss going over and over again, on around the mouth and practicing. Moved up over onto the boy is the friend covering his body over, the younger almost completely in heaviness at times, the images one on top of one another like pictures out around the bed in the back part, when no one appeared to be looking, appear to be life spread in them like now come alive.

PART TWO

57.

It is faces that made people want to see more of the story of the boys with horror, after the having been taken in. Wait until you saw the faces, the littlest one looking about like eight or ten only, not even his age.

Just wait until you saw pictures of the actual house.

Groups of men would come together in circles, before going back over the boys. In a small room the boys would be made as comfortable as possible, black shoes cold leather shining all around them. They would turn back and forth, move towards then walk away.

There were jobs like this one where the heart could not always be breaking.

58.

From the moment one goes away, there were these things to be thinking about, though one way through the years would be to try not to think about it too much. The friend would speak up, in days following. Only because he has seen how the boys needed so much help, only so he could give them all he could, everything he had to give and could, everything he could do but nothing outside of what he should, when he opened up the trailer to them that night. He would take the stand saying how much he loved those boys, saying how he was going to try to make a home for them, saying how he would do anything for them, there those days in court in a gray suit.

The friend would be booked, too, not to worry about that. He was not going to be getting out for a very long time or back there, a face drained, drawn in later pictures, like he now saw what happens with what you say to them.

59.

If the situation were to be controlled, no evidence left, everything has to burn away. The boys knew what needed to be done, just hadn't known when, how exactly to go about it.

They needed a thing that was going to spark that was going to make the whole place ignite up a lot more bigger than normal flames if they wanted to try to make all the way burn the whole place. Nothing more left for developing but the "action." The older would keep moving on to next steps, like he knew doing what they both wanted, didn't they. They would need something like a hammer. They still had to be quiet while they were looking for something like that. The father might still be looking for them, if not. If found, if forced back there, they wanted there to be no chance for him to try to do anything with them, threaten them, and they had someone to help them, someone going to treat them better?

Who started it, getting it to the point where what happened was the boy fell across there in the way trying to run, the father coming after him, the father would begin that night to see what was happening, happening to him, knocking him then all what further into what dark. Pulling at him, pushing him from behind a shoulder. Not bleeding or anything, not yet he's not. Grabbed at him, to catch him by the hair, shaking him to make these marks here along neck, the arm. The boys know how they have to get away, they say, if they want to leave for good, to finally never be brought back to seeing him again. When he isn't there they believe then nobody would mess with them, boys said things like how it makes no difference to them if the "father" were to be dead, and how happy they both would be to never have to again see him.

They agreed how they are tired of him, looking at them the way he did, his never stopping trying to see everything.

When his brother hit him, hit him hard, harder even than he had ever yet himself been.

60.

If some things were said, none of them would ever be getting out, something to think about, before a stand is taken, and once questioning started.

The voices of the boys could not waver when speaking, as if trained to think the way they have, say what they will. Boys can always stand up a little taller, when important, respected men are to be speaking to them. When the boys are to be brought in, they would be made comfortable. They would wait there, while questions were asked, be given drinks, and there would be more, when finished with those.

Then a next one would take over. The younger trying to curl around himself with his hands, he would go into no more detail, what they had planned, how much all along, and then who would appear to be in control more, just how much given the way he would sit back in his chair, that there in that court after back room they go into arguing who it is should be going away, one or two or how many responsible that would have to be found, one night he snaps, and they would have to defend themselves. Lips pink, saying how he was going to do those things for the both of them? He would do whatever he wanted for him? Men with their bodies that would bulk around everyone there, filing in to be grouped together all, everyone rising for a reading of who is the darker one and fairer.

61.

It would be that way unless he did something about it. Important to think about is going silent. Not just the TV in the other room neighbors could see if they really looked. The father wanted it said anyone should see how much he loved those boys.

It was no more than a dull light inside, the TV dimmed.

He wanted them getting into their beds, even if they weren't sleepy yet. He would come back there in a minute, to look at things, then another. He would be the one who gets to look at them, any way he wanted.

He comes back there again, for nights.

62.

This was what they were going to have to do. Wait for him to go off to some payphone again, to leave again, say he was doing that. The night they were just going to do it. He follows behind him, watching while he looks. It needs to look like someone has tried to break in, to take what little they had there and to hurt them. If he were not sleeping, he could fight against seeing it coming. His brother has been getting prepared. Something still on the TV, turned down so he could be trying to listen out for the boys, a bit but not shut off completely. He sees now. It was late at night, after he was in there with the paper, rustling shifted about, tossing some up over onto the couch in reach of the armchair.

Is what it would have to be like, the father saying how he would take the whole house apart if he had to, if the boys didn't start listening, they wouldn't cooperate, wouldn't tell him, if they ever wanted out again.

He was in the chair, if not already moved over to the couch, chair sat almost in the center of the room. Currents that keep going across the face. They won't wait around to watch them stop, the mouth to open up just a bit more, the sound to move down low then up the body for a while keep going through it behind lids, still there in the chair and the only light close over it from the TV.

63.

Legs opened moved down to rest.

In these stretches of nobody, they were going to learn to be more together.

Tell a boy he needed to be taken better care of, and it was not surprising when he started believing that.

So he was going to have to be in better control.

He has his eye on things, he says. They were going to learn how he was the one. He was the one to tell them when they had both done something wrong.

64.

The father would not let them stay there any longer. He comes back one night from down at the end of the trailer. The father pulls off, driving quicker. Rates on the radio, station inside the car, dins around, old speakers coming in and out and saying how if the boys don't learn this car was something they were going to have to get rid of, if the boys didn't learn better. Having left them there with him, when it's offered, there was no reason for the one to be back there in the friend's bedroom. He said they're going. When starting to see the look made on faces, the younger boy beginning almost to pout, mouth opened getting ready like about to say something. Right then get up. Nobody wanted to get up in the front with him? News, even though there was singing.

65.

When the car pulled up, break gets pulled, complaints things dug in, heavy door shut in the driveway, boots heard going over the gravel front outside, the place to park.

Is that what the neighbors heard, the older yelling to the father that man was no such thing, they hated him, both the boys do?

Curtains, too, then are made to move so it looks like at times the place itself can be breathing. Metal frames around the hallowed supposedly. The boys are brought back after trying to run away again, during one of the last of the few weeks they would all spend together, but the neighbors next door say they heard no fights over there, nothing coming out from the yard up to the edge of the windows, no voice not really yelling for the boys to get back in there.

It doesn't matter what you thought you heard outside, when the TV was on. One needs time away, from the things that could enthrall, away from the things that disturb. They would go through this together as a family, working together, the father said.

There was a change of mood, it appears, that stretched around the house, down into the living room, broken in a few good days that would not last much longer. They had apparently begun decorating, trying to do such, with the holidays coming up. Trying, appealing to them, especially this time of year, it was important. They would go through this together as a family, working together the father said. Looked like he was trying to do some renovations, the father getting things prepared some weekends for the other projects.

66.

What would help them get up near to him without being heard is the TV, chair a pattern of russet orange-brown, dyed, that could be pushed back better for sleeping. Liked to prop his feet up on the couch. Cold food is there on the plate next to him, the "father" so-called, hours since they have last been seen over at the other place. The boys were afraid of what was going to be happening to them. If they didn't do what he said. After this night, the last one, nothing was going to be back there, waiting there. They would be able to leave, then. Like a slap, right back in the face was what it was going to have to be like. What is picked up then would be by chance, what was left there in the house, the hall, since the last of so many times they had run away all the knives in the house they made sure to take with them.

First the brother was going to move the coffee cup, before hitting has to start, before he woke up. The younger watched him picking it up, the breathing being heard so loudly. Some things they are going to take care of themselves. It would feel close to sleep, like never having to go back there. Come into the hallway, his older brother still holding it.

67.

In the morning, the boys are there with heads down between their arms, and they wouldn't look up, when being told by him how he wanted to see their eyes. They were going to cooperate those boys, he said. Couldn't always have whatever you wanted. Not that day right then they couldn't. The older asks again for something for breakfast. Didn't work that way. Where there were old walls would be put up new. Why was it dark there, all around his eyes? What was that rubbing there again?

Look at him, the father trying to say he wanted them to know how he knows. Other people find it easy enough to say how, one day, if things were bad then they were going to get better. What was wrong with being happy there with him, the father wanted to know, waiting for it to clear. It would only take some patience. Things could always be a lot worse.

Whatever was taking place somewhere else would always be better, wouldn't it? Those boys didn't even when asked want to come sit in the living room with their own father?

He would call for them to bring out whatever they were doing back there, while he picked up newspapers from around the couch, the floor, around his chair, pitched them up onto where he wanted them to sit. Both of the boys back there. Wanted to talk to them. All the next day the father wanted them doing, school things, and all the rest of the next one, if they were finished with those already, he would find something else for them to work on.

His big hand clicked around the sound, another few channels over the week's sports and weather, like he always did for himself, a late night dinner across from it. It flickered against walls, made them look different colors in the light. He reaches over for the remote, and thinking how they might get rid of it, the space that gave.

That day, right then, it was going to stay unplugged. All that was on there was all they weren't really like. All three of them in the house needed to start practicing being quieter together.

He wants them to come sit in front of him. A smaller room was going to be for it, one he'd already painted all green. First, he asked the older to go put back in the kitchen the painting supplies.

They go next to the door, thinner for later, tops put back on tight. A baseball bat had been brought in, for keeping in the hall, metal for the friend, he says. A lot of damage could be done with one. That's why you make sure no one was standing behind you when you go to swing, the area cleared, before slinging to the side one on a playground. Or one is kept hidden under the bed for that, like their father said, if the friend ever tried to do anything again, get inside to see any of them.

68.

Those nights that would go into days, weeks into months, when they were being held, there would be no way for the friend to watch out for them anymore, and the boys would be moved on to a bigger place, where there would be thinking to be done about what could still happen, if they cooperated, what they could still go on to do. Legs in long pants bend to sit, mouths above move. Slacks, saying something, talking then standing, door opened and then sound from next door, more light.

There is a room where "interrogations" is what happens. It is where they are going to have to be until morning, together in the one room to listen to their consciences, the words they knew. It was where the boys would have to learn something inside their selves. All of them together, the boys would not look at the father, when he was talking to them, before he plugs back in the TV. They would have to live there, he was saying, and how he was going to have to get stricter. He wouldn't stop saying how he didn't want them ever outside of the house without him. He's seen the way the two of them were becoming, he would not stop saying. They would be watched, watching them still every single second keeping them there. Hours they'd be inside there, being careful what came out of mouths.

69.

There was a special kind of punishment he had for them, for when he felt like they needed to be all together more, for when staying with him there in that place does not seem good enough anymore. When he was looking at them the way he does, it is only about discipline, he says. There in the house, the three of them as a family were going to be looking at each other as long as he wanted them sitting in the one room with him. Then they might not even need to talk about it anymore.

There would be no one to see those nights held silent and dark, time for going in there. He would make them go into the side room, one smaller than one made for sleeping, a green boxed-in space set aside, a room where against the wall a face feels crushed in. He has a chair there, too.

Many nights they would go in there, sit, to be looked at over across from him. He doesn't want to see them moving from in there, only find them here, doesn't want them moving. He wants to be seeing how neither one of them had gone away. If they just said what they knew, everything would be fine, like he had told them. Then they might be able to leave the house. They know what he wants to know. Before everything goes wrong the last time, they would sit there until the sun comes up, he's thinking. He would tell them when they could move, when it was both of them he felt had had enough.

He got them out of bed for it. If both of them cooperated, then they could go back to it, only once they had learned to start acting better like they should.

Some nights it was after it had gotten darker they were moved in there, pushed along, the father's voice pulling at them telling them to move, when expressions on a face couldn't be seen, not anymore, the house so dark with the father looking at them both, waiting for them until broken, for a day when he felt like he could still speak to them again, silence to yield. Then it comes more regularly, some nights a bit before anything to eat. Sometimes the fingers and their joints on the thighs of his jeans start looking bruised, when it goes on until morning. It got lighter over nicks from work not yet scabbed over, a few new now and then. Tells them to sit up straighter, like the morning is not now going to be the time for acting any differently.

He would keep them for a long time at the kitchen table, trying to keep them in the house before the day began, and wanting them to tell him before going out what they were so ashamed about? They could sleep when they got back home from school. Must be something if they wouldn't say. If he was leaving out of the house, even for a minute, they would be coming with him.

Had to understand they could not just do whatever they wanted. It is why there were laws. Once they reached the age of sixteen, they would be adults. Then they could live wherever they wanted, happily. Leave then, if they want, do whatever. But not until.

Until then, he would raise them the way he knows how, the father said. They would be watched. They heard? They understood?

70.

Another night he wanted them up, but the boys don't want to come back out there, not after the last time he tried to get them to say, tell him what he wants to hear only, all that looking at him the right way.

Words fill up a head in the little bit of closed off room. They know what's been done to them, don't they, don't those boys?

So doesn't want to hear anymore about it. Entire weekends they would not be talking sometimes, not saying another word. It depends on what he says. Not until the father was ready to say get up. Not until he said. He wanted them being as still as possible, arms down to sides, rawboned, kept trying to straighten them up.

The chair gets pulled up closer, lines around the eyes seen. In the room, it was quiet silence and breathing just, the rule being for the boys to look at him, when he leaned forward, there only at his face, not yet snapping yet staring. He stood up over them and then got closer down next to their necks, faces, into them. None of the things in the house broken yet, stove still working and TV too, just unplugged. What is he going to do with them? Tell him? Asked look up now, made them do the breathing out for him and pulling at their clothes to smell them, too. He needed to be sure, the father said.

If he had to guard over them, that was how it was going to be.

He would wedge a kitchen chair against the door to block the way.

All will be quiet but for a sound in the throat, chest, and those boys there against each other being, toward sleep then brushed, question become how he was going to keep them in the house, evenings with him in that green room after a few days before the last they tried to run again, and he caught them out in the yard, out where they know they weren't supposed to be.

71.

Members of the extended family would appear for later developments, comments. The one who had been helping, they don't want him getting away, either. They know what they've been doing, both those boys. What kind of a life was this. You imagined one like you might one day have.

72.

It couldn't be told what he must have been thinking, so they had to stay there, where the younger believes he can save it by not saying anything.

At school, there are other names for it, other words they say, but nobody is going to make him open his eyes again on the bus one day. Nights it got so late there sitting things start happening inside a head, the younger seeing clearly how the father is going to hurt them, way he keeps looking at them, eyes darker even in the morning, the father saying how he sees those looks those two sometimes got together.

Look at him the way they do. Keep very still there, thinking, with the older beside him, both mouths opening like wanting to say something, and then the look on faces caved in, around to expressions blanker even than before.

At night, silence is such days it was hard to think, weight of the couch pressed up underneath coming back, and still his saying they are going to "talk," soon as the father got home, to think about what they had all been clearly feeling.

73.

You let him do this to you?

No, he never touched them any other way. No, never with a hand or fist just those nights eyes.

It was mental abuse, the friend told him. Not until he said they could. They had to answer only with his being the way he was what they knew he wanted to hear.

74.

It was those nights he looked wrong in the chair, shades of the wall bled up against, the house that in sleep leaned a quiet over the whole they were supposed to be jarred inside, lights on a face back awake changed. A shape curving away.

He was the only reason they had to keep being there. The older tried looking at the wall, up there behind shadows, stomach knotted, glare on the greening shimmering burnished, a water spot, palmetto.

Squeak of the chair's wood with the slight shifts, his nodding head down to sleep. They weren't going to call him by that anymore, they decided, euphemism, the head of that man the "father" giving a little twitch or two more to itself.

75.

The older boy would not be able to keep something like a grin from starting on his face, when they were taken into the court. There, in some of the pictures the younger would appear leaning almost on the arm of a lawyer, in others forward against the table. When the younger sits up straight, his head goes almost to the start of a man's shoulder, eyes held all around, the younger and him.

Try to do the thing with your face, when taken in there, make it look right. Try to meet those stares when speaking, and evidence anyone could see.

High above them it would buzz, its one eye to watch turning, scanned over like it could bear down inside heads. Dumb, and cruel, voices in a room say before even one mouth was opened. It would take time to be sorry, for any crying. More and more pictures. What everyone wanted to see in the eyes was how they were. They would want to see them putting their hands up in front of faces. On the cover of one of the published accounts to come, the boys look up at the corner where a camera gets angled, leaning again over an interrogation table. Pictures are there too in the paper for drawing a reader in, as stories under headlines go off to be reviewed mornings before coffee, further away.

Did you remember such a story, or think so, this story starting how young both of them were, and how they looked so young at the time, one thing a matter is made of repeatedly, as they would be later in words described again. When not from the right kinds of families, boys needed help. It would look best if there would be a new shirt for each day of the week, weeks in a court that would go by slow, news catching up around on other stations, as sources attempted to bring them home just as safely as they could be borne.

76.

How old was he again? Everybody would want to know. They would have to trust the attorneys, like they had trusted him. That is if they didn't want to find themselves for the rest of conceivable lives in some prison. Where were they when it happened? Each boy knows what each to say.

No matter what is said out the mouth, think back in the mind.

77.

Yes. Remembering. Because of the way he pushed him up against a wall, the youngest would say. Before he pinned him down and wouldn't let him get up. They would say how he had snapped this night and they had to defend themselves, the younger down on the floor is wrestled there, he is trying to keep him there, where they are afraid something worse than normal is going to this once happen. After looking at him the way he started looking at the both of them, the youngest, the father gets up to go after him. It is why they had to try to keep getting out of there, keep trying to run going away from him.

It was worse that night than it had ever been. It was not just once he pushed him in there between rooms of the house, they would say, he would be pushing him way too much, pushing way too hard out of the other into the living, especially the weaker, pushed him up against the back like that to get him in there, the house, pulling him from behind his shoulder, sometimes he would, his head knocking up against the frame of the one door green, he doesn't want to go in. That's what had showed them they had to get away from him out there in the other room or it just keeps happening.

78.

The night they were reminded again in the car. They should know, the boys should remember. That's all the father would say right then. The friend thinks he is the one and only? The night it was going to happen, the father was taking them over somewhere else then.

He needs to see somebody, but they weren't going to see that one anymore.

The father has been invited many, many times. They think there is only one place, but there is another for all of them, the friend probably thinking it was going to be just another night he was going to get to see them.

There were not many people, but still a couple outside of work. Somewhere they could stay awhile, while he talks for some advice how to make the boys see reason, the house someone they've seen around the flea market.

He's saying he doesn't know what to do with them at all.

He's been thinking about it, weeknights, falling asleep in the one chair only his chair. If the boys run away again, he knows always the first person they would go to, and where gone before to get some help, who to call from the station up the street, what's going to happen next when looking. Call somebody, if the father wanted to get another opinion.

He's got to tell somebody. At first think it is what tonight is about accomplishing.

Couldn't matter how the house and yard were finally getting to look one way. An idea in the father's head spits around and around.

Couldn't matter how the older just got back there, how the father had them both again, how much he wanted it.

Go find what they could in the back room of this new place to get into. Or they see the swing outside? Go outside if they wanted, so they could talk alone.

Both men reached down going for their beers. The father doesn't know if he could tell it all to this one, not while the boys were still right there, down the hall. They'll play outside. There was this thing the father was thinking, how they were probably going to have to move somewhere else, somewhere far away. They wouldn't be seeing some people ever again. Once they get away, he believes things can change.

79.

He sees how he took it all in over there. There was something else strange, once it was being thought about later, besides just this fact of their all having come over. The one boy he had seen before, head down, mumbling around at the flea market, usual soft-spoken. "Daddy," he wasn't saying, called him by a name. That was one thing that he could remember.

At some point the older zipped his jacket back on. The youngest, like his father, he had wanted to keep his on. Could they go outside? In the backyard, there is a porch swing setup. Once the boys are no longer inside their father begins his really trying to say.

It starts like a joke, but he said there was something he was really afraid about. With the boys, he meant. Thinking maybe there was no one he could trust, with what all he needed to tell somebody, shifting there on a new couch, soft, could lean back on it. With the friend they've started to scare him a bit. What he needs is for the way they were acting, being, to stop. The boys think now they know everything too.

He's seen some things, some things others wouldn't believe. They're planning something, all of them together. He sees it on their faces, anytime he looks in on them, looking up quickly, then down again.

80.

The hall to step into was a short one, when he wanted to see why it was the house seemed feeling the way it was, with the boys spending time together in the one bedroom whispering. That night or the next, when it was the only way, and they had to find the right spot, would he do it? Would he take up for him? It would be that day, or the next, the only way. They're whispering back there, talking like it back there little louder in excitement built up some nights before bed, like boys did, even at twelve and thirteen, how they were going to get out. Otherwise, normally quiet. He would be coming back there to see what all the whispering was about, hearing them talking in voices dulled by night light, and when they got excited, voices slipping up into other registers he didn't want to live with him anymore either, always asking about it, him. They weren't going to see anyone, he'd be saying, especially the friend.

One thing he knew for sure, there was going to be no more listening to the kind of music that would play in the bedroom like moaning sometimes, a kind of animal sung heat. It was why he first had unplugged everything in the house, so they would listen to him, and after that, wanted only quiet. He would turn everything back on when he was ready. He knew what they liked watching over there, inside with that one. He'd see hands down in their laps, like they were playing a game, no more. Not until he said it was OK. They sat themselves down there in front of the TV. You wouldn't want to think about these sorts of things seen, on all the equipment that lay around the trailer, stuff from so long ago, some of it is, has to be, even on old tapes, discs, boys with bodies like theirs still played. He knew what they'd been trying to watch, he said, when he was not in there watching over them.

81.

It was closer to midnight, getting later, some shadow less distinct, and the night darkening in around everything. Didn't look like they were doing anything wrong. The boys looked fine to him, out there talking in the yard, when seen in the back, out the window, though harder to see. Just a few more beers left. It was getting late, though, for boys to be out there. They would come in at points in the night from out in the yard to ask about something to eat.

So much of it that night sounded like a joke, might, until you looked at his face. Some of the things he is saying the boys were going to have to do without, how he thought it was going to have to be. One thing that could still be taken away was the TV. It was shut on and off. He only wanted them to see how hard he has been working, so they had this place to live. He was going to make it where they could never lock any of the rooms inside, when playing, they say, so he's taken handles off of some of the doors completely. He wants the door to the bedroom kept open, especially at night when they are supposed to be sleeping. He can hear then if they are staying in bed or not. Both boys have to learn acting better, to be where they were supposed to be.

Some nights from the doorways he would watch in the stillness. One night, the flashlight, and there is a bag at home in the kitchen, alongside supplies for the house painting they kept asking about. They needed to make it look nicer. It's filled with new locks. More painting another night when he gets home, once he got everything they needed. He had even told them they could pick out some colors, living room a shade not calming either, nettles, and hard to think of any other color for it all to be, other than what it already was.

Locks, even for the bedrooms. He would be the one with the keys. Don't worry about how he was going to take care of them he said. He had gone to the store for these and other materials. He would put a new lock on the back. It was not something to look away from, once it got noticed. Last time it was the deadbolt for the front door. He was only letting himself sleep late at night positioned in the front room, even make it feel like a prison if he had to, threatened.

82.

The men who would guard over boys, thinking they were going to be better off stating what being told, swore things to an effect of many times. The men would come up to them, and down into their faces, all those bodies that would circle around them, the desks and chairs metal and wood joints that sound popping. They know what the boys needed, what they called "motivation," in a room that got even greener looking before dark bled through.

83.

Back inside, out one's kitchen, when the curtains moved aside the boys could still be seen, blurring out around the back swing, the boys still stretching legs. He was sure they were both involved in things he had to show someone, another light clicking on. The older, it was just the way he looks at him. Seemed like he's just gotten them back from the last time they tried to run away. He saw the way he looked at him. It wasn't only getting away from him.

Anyone might happen to see, on the way out to around the car, if they happened to see in his eyes, or heard out the window around coming in and out, how he was getting more nervous, a little more ready to admit to someone the nature of how the boys had begun breaking him down. There was more to what he needed to talk about.

You had no idea, he said, of the things a boy is not supposed to know about yet. Impressions he was having at first, just these hunches. He saw how the turning on him had started. Then the idea crawled in more fully, how he needed better to look out. He put the younger in his own bedroom, where the father himself had been sleeping, before the older, keeping the two boys away from each other at night so they wouldn't keep saying all the things to each other they do. Blanket and pillow on the couch are for the father, at points in the night he checks at each door inside and to the outside. He would come back there until they were each finally sleeping and until there was quiet, no more interference of any kind. Silence collected around cans emptying.

84.

Could he become that kind of friend, if this new one was someone he could really come to with all this? He needed to show it to someone, see what someone else might think. But he knows it was getting late.

You want another?

He's not saying he's the kind of person who would normally look at something like this it's just that he needed some help. Out in the trunk were some pictures that had already been taken. These pictures are not ones soon to appear in papers, and not candid ones of the Christmas faces, inserted into paperback middles beside mug shots. The father had thought how he should take some of his own, if they ever tried to leave again he'd have most recent ones for copies to put around and for police, like keeping little pieces of his son, separate from other pictures. Anyone who might be like the friend, wanted to, could look. He put his hand back into the carpeted well of the car. See? He's saying he doesn't know how far it had gone, maturing slightly, but still not enough, he was going to make sure it went no further. Nothing would be left there the next time the friend wanted to go into the trailer back for his shiny stack.

It had been hard to see some things just by passing by the bedroom, walking down the paneled hallway, but once he's gone more inside there, and started looking around, stepped in it, there at night where the friend slept, pictures and pages of them around on the side of the bed where he slept, a load and hoard of youngness, some he himself must have taken, made happen. In the car back, no, it's not right. No, he doesn't want to see what's tucked away. Up on a computer, too. He must have been there, just before or just after. He doesn't really look. Right there, close at hand, see how he has him arranged in one?

85.

In one of them, something held in hand looks through angles of flashes a white smear, but that there could be knee it looked loomed out, and lighting a cream colored landscape, so close like that to skin but in another more moved onto back, and more arranged, in one, focus all gone washed out there too, much pressed up against been. One time he remembers something distinctly about getting a picture of the boy's teeth, a tooth was loose. This way he remembers again another time he was sitting up there without him, the two of them together. Coming back over other days when they should get going, boys need to eat, how often they should come over. He's got to take more when they get home, in case they stay gone longer next time.

Light rendered close the tiny muscles around a boy's mouth, way it got held. Some of the pictures showed nothing above neck, milked skin still even. Didn't have to be his necessarily, but there are drawers full over there. What does a boy think? You could see just a back in another, cheeks losing a last bit of roundness.

86.

How hard it was to be alone with him with everything he wanted to feel, wanted done. And there were things his boy wrote, found in his room,the notebook full.

87.

At first the younger hadn't understood all the things his brother said to him, all the ideas he gets in his head when brought back. Just because he's always called him one thing, that doesn't mean he has to keep on with it. Doesn't mean anything. Maybe he is no such thing. They could both be anyone's boys, an idea he gets from somewhere. He has been trying to say how if they have more brothers other places, these half-ones even they know can they, how could they, even be sure this man they had always to go back to was really their father?

The older had promised, back in the bedroom. He said how he was going to be there for the one they both knew was the weaker of two. Not to worry. To protect the younger, before things got even worse, someone was going to have to do something, give a man like the one who always said he was their father what he had coming. The boys know what they have to do, and then they wouldn't be coming home to him saying anything anymore.

88.

What happens next then is strange, later it's reported. The boys come in to make a show of affection for him in the new place, almost like they are showing off. As much as any outsider could tell, that night the boys act happy, grab at the camouflage jacket the father is wearing, leaving on, that night over there, holding onto him.

Both gather round closer with tighter hugs on the body, holds clinging touching up on the body, and then they keep calling the father repeatedly by first name. He's trying to talk. They keep holding on, both, not just the younger, when he asks them to go back outside for just a little longer. They go up to him on the couch, keep trying to wrap their arms around him while sitting there together still on the couch. Stuff like that. Laughing, they joke, tugging at the loops of his jeans and saying how loose they are getting, his pants, he needs to start wearing a belt because of all the weight he's losing, and the boys start even then to kiss him. One or two aimed at cheeks, his neck, up near around the father's ear, and he tries to brush them off, saying they were talking, but not saying much.

89.

Come morning, they would drive away in the car that got beat-up a bit more along the way down the road. When they left, they would clear out towards road signs and exits, closer there to one, before that one too passed along paving, going by again in the car rusting, yellow and white lines accumulating, others down, a few with headlights still on, down the road passing. Others whistle by, cars going around that get bigger, better, bigger. The car swung into a turn, and he'd roll down the window when he was ready. Nobody wanted to get up in the front with him?

In the back of the car, it got much hotter down in darker parts, boys with their knees kept hitting up against the back of the seat, tapping. They don't know what to do with their hands. They should not sit so close together back there. The father doesn't want to see more of that way he's looking at him in the rearview mirror. Ashamed of what they've been doing, aren't they, and that was why at some point the one started crying? He knows the reason why he wanted them over there all the time. Know where you wanted to go, the father said. When they got home, it would be for looking over in the room, one of those sessions together, a little more time before bed.

90.

Around some time after midnight, it started to sound like more crying. The older couldn't tell if the sound was in the other room, his brother, or only the TV coming back on, the sounds around the TV after finished eating, shifting around in the nose, mouth, chest flecked, that man. The night it was all going to be over with, the younger is twelve, his brother older by a year. Sleeping there with eyes opened up quickly against any presence near the chair. It would be the very next time he even looks like he is about to even lay a hand on the head of the littler, they'd already said, try to even touch his brother again, keep going at him how they all know. He would go right for his face. The chin rocks against chest bone, a clack that's made deeper. A little tap was not going to hurt him, so going at it until he would not be getting up out of the chair anymore, until too tired to hit at him anymore, and hands older couldn't hold anymore, not getting up into there the chair anymore, picture in front of the eyes slammed from front, didn't get off all on top of him.

The boy starts yelling, crying how he needs his brother. It was a lonely place inside a head, arm yanking how he always saw it in the light, too. He'd come into the room when he called him. What he was wearing that night he got what was coming was the same as any other, there in a camouflage hat, jacket over white t, blue jeans, hole in one of the socks.

91.

The older boy wasn't even looking anymore for a hammer, to strike the blows with whatever, when his brother sees him getting the bat, bigger. The brother would have it. He wasn't going to. He'd have it in one hand then move it to the other, settled weight against hollowed cupping, light lobbing against palm, choked up high on a quiet test seen somewhere like this before, a little harder hand connections practicing that would land in plate cracks. The little barely blinks whatever hurting inside. Pushed way too much. One learns not to care by not further thinking. The brother comes in and goes right at the face, and the only place any hurt could live. Did he get pushed? Where in the head doesn't have to be like them before, when thinking what could be done, how they'd have to live with him, forever, it. He sits there in front of them talking always like the boss. Isn't going to anymore once it is thought if just this one thing was done everything would change.

92.

His brother hit him square on. He hit the body in the chair solid first head-on from the front, facing, a connection forward knocked out of the mouth a dull little moan. Around the base of the bat his brother squeezed tighter shaking in his arms and then hit him again, a number of times, though not yet ten. He slipped, and the body in the chair jerked under swinging under him. He could try to move then, gathered in patches slowed through skin open already colored, did not matter, after only one or two hits, and mouth stretched already, running already, and again he twisted before it all became one more throe he would not be looking back from.

He hit off once to the side, swung again, missed, again tried more shaky then half-hearted before more confident, tightening both arms, holding on to do it ten or so, dozen nearly more connections to tire face, head, feeling all along the body it then.

93.

See there is no way, no way outside the house, no way all three sets go to wield it, for hands to have wrapped all equally around, hit him in the head until he doesn't move at all anymore and the brain presses against the hands. Everyone was going to see what the hands had been used for, what the hands had done. Few and far removed, too, come the noises from the mouth. It sounds at some points inside like gum popping. They'd leave him how they found him, when they were done prop him up. In all actuality it only takes about five minutes to do dying.

Swung harder, muscles not feeling a thing, adjusted his stance striking against the hole again deepening wet sounds he plants, slapped up and down unstuck. Some sprayed over onto the lamp, high up in places as the ceiling, then the floor wet, behind the chair it patters and pools but nobody gets a chance to look there, the pile soaked through from brown to black gone everywhere sprayed out the cave used to see, the older keeps hitting him or he'll come after them, some more slipped before the face broke there, next to scalp, nose torn open, chest bruised along neck, sounds like a wolf crying. There, that's all he ever was.

94.

Maybe ten times, he'd have to later say. Quick, slight, pauses between metal against skin and bone, so he could just move a bit more, him trying to breathe, along the line of swings ceasing, to get up in quick gasps, another breath caught.

95.

When the older had finished what he'd done to him, he held still the bat, took it with him running into the bigger, master bedroom for throwing down there. They had to make sure the house starts to burn, behind. They'd burn it from the inside, anything they could find to make the fire go faster collected, so that could get more out of control, that would make it just burn to the ground. A number of things would help, he knows. It is all worked out from having played with it before, a fire that could get hot enough to melt even metal.

In the middle of the bed in the room with the littlest it lands softly, end with the stuff on it. The littlest just stood there watching. First it gets very warm. All around needs to be burning. Be sure everything is left behind that needs to be gotten rid of, thinner splashing, all over their shoes, when having to get out quick. They had to run out, quick, before it starts taking over the bedroom.

It was harder for the younger to breathe, still, after they'd gone through yards crisscrossed against a pattern, there where the trees begin to ring. Even this late, something in a tree was still trying to believe it could sing. When they got to the next tree, a few things low hum inside, closer to the paved parts before taking off, and they would be coming for them, they would be looked for, everyone looking for them. Muscles in the legs hurt in the head. Keep going telling breathing to shut up. Further down a road, towards the ends of other blocks, more sound windows around who, how, would be coming for the boys.

Something worse than normal was going to happen this time, why they had to keep running, get out of there.

96.

Uniforms on, they walk around outside on the rounds, shoes in halls tracking down to duller thudding. Not overnight are defenses built. Others with keys walk down long halls, sound pounding others, walking by rooms kept getting closed, walls walked up against. Not all of the boys did want it, they say. A band of sweat stripes down in back along one shirt tucked in. Reiteration is more staccato, more pointed. Boys say how he'd done it to them without them wanting it. He hasn't. Others making sure everyone was being kept safe they say move along on a list of duties, before the errands on the way home. Not ready to give up on the friend? Not yet?

97.

The fire should be allowed to take its course in places, while also being controlled, curbed, and blocked, as much as those whose job it was were able to, then, more of a continuing on through of a home gone alight was done, tour through what had apparently become a scene of crime, news spread. Before too long, something like this would be, if he kept it up, a story that would make it into all the papers, mark the words. One of those days, boys like the two of them they would be sitting there for the next set of questions.

Only if he'd acted right could the friend's mother go peacefully. Something he had to know was how one day she was going to die like everybody else. Promise he wouldn't go getting himself one day locked up once she was no longer there someone to watch out for him? Always said how next time a sentence wouldn't be so light.

Up and down around there, voices that night said things like asking mothers to come look. Nicer houses even people were no longer inside of anymore after the lights, then shadows that stretch out long across lawns. A small fire, that's all it was. Nothing really major, once it'd been safely put out. Lights then before too long mixed flashing over skin and broken-in sirens with hot, cold sound, boys that brought authorities over radios, searching, leading out for the two of them, before they'd get away.

Knocking so loud only because of the job the officers have to do.

Go get back in your bed.

Go, do what they said, the glass of another door screen rattled, looked through locked.

98.

It was because of the eyes then that arms look that way, stung in running legs more because they couldn't either one stop moving. They couldn't run that night much further, all the way over to the trailer, to find him. He's not about to start crying.

When he couldn't run anymore, they just have to walk then, fast as possible, slowed down, fanned under a low canopy of limbs, little brother's legs shorter ones while he tries breathing again in gulps moves more forward, out there into the night they won't be going back from. Even the jacket left, remember that thing the friend said. Tell him wherever they'd be, wherever either of them want him to come get them, just call. He'd come pick them up as soon as he could, he'd offered, said anytime, he would be there waiting for them, whenever they need him, and they don't have to worry ever about bringing anything with them. There would be new things.

Once, not too long ago, when it was still of some use to wish for what one wanted, once there were those who believed they would find themselves in their rightful places in the end, everything that had been coming to them all along there finally for the taking. Once those boys really did live.

The boys rounded the corner of another house. When firemen get there, it would be seen how this time they had gone missing again, they must have locked up behind them, leaving the place to burning, though it would not get very far. The house would still be all shut up, front door and back locked, all windows not yet broken or burst in. The boys get further down a street over where no one is yet at any doors, or there to the sides of any windows. Everybody would be looking, but they couldn't be seen by anyone. No matter what, keep going. No one in the yards yet, past streets where neighbors, some would, gather to watch soon the lights on lawn excuses, coming out pulling things on over robes, nightclothes, feeling like they've got to go out, see.

They were still running at least to a place where bigger roads start finally, after side ones of no signs but only a few cars. If they don't keep going, whatever is behind them then is going to catch up with them. Only once they are far enough away can they chance anything more. They have to get off to more trees, there where it's more pronounced, and the gum goes up and down them, boys there down in other bushes before moved back into the buckthorn, gone further down a way the road along, and skin still wet and cooling, feeling colder after the running. They get more time where there is silence more, back there behind one of the gas stations. Remembering what they needed to do next. Just a bit more they'll run to move along to the phone, too long and it will be too late and too light, cars on the two-lane hum along where the roads met others before veering. He's thinking about getting back to the trailer, trying that.

Or someone will already be waiting for them in a tiny bit of woods that starts there, where they will have to keep quiet. Everything would be all ready, all waiting for them. Whatever they want. The building itself looks like it shut on and off, ceasing brightly behind there, passing cars sound around the boys covered in red leaves of ash.

The payphones still work out a way across from gas pumps, yellow rubber in degrees slick of sweat up against the ear, where what is a song about apples riffs through speakers under the tin overhang, green fluorescents lighting the way. The place open twenty-four hours, the boy inside circle sign winks on and off, green, red, lit up drink machines and the shelves inside lined up with things to eat. The girl behind the counter before the cigarettes would call the police, without a doubt, if either walked into the bright area around front, and something is seen wrong with them.

99.

The gas station they were behind was named for a book for kids. The smaller he is in the story, more manageable, and the family has been praying for a little boy, the pages turned to see it happen again and again. The boy is born just like they wanted him to be, they believed, until he devised his plan for going free. Things grew up there between the pages of magazines, covers stripped off mass-markets, moralizers with their gems (*Because Daddy is a king, not a prince. And kings know what must be done—even if it's hard—to make things right*), the bestselling of a Dr. Oz, out of date small-time dailies, the wet boxes goods arrived in there further away from the steel design of the one dumpster.

He was not there already waiting. They need the phone back around there in front. No stars in outlines above leather leaves, wrappers shine silver near tall trees. Keep calling, even if he doesn't get him the first time.

They would hide out there where it begins to sap for those first days, the boys believed, if need be. They believed they could stay until safe to come back out from there again, until the older found somewhere else to go, not thinking clearly mumbling there were things they were going to need even to stay a night.

It's along the surface the father made him well, the younger will say of something that's scratched him, some branch. That's how he handled him. If anyone tried to say anything, the boy has here on the wrist the proof he says where the blood dotted up wiped along his jeans coarsely back and forth to further aggravate punctures' small openings. The boys try to rub spots on their clothes against dirt there, stones, to try to get it off, rub on their hands more leaves, watching a clearing, as far as they can see looking, clinks between some breathing again, car lights shine there the road that loops. When pulling up headlights could be brights belonging to anyone around there, shining out, out towards the ends of the asphalt. But the car shadow his, they manage to step out towards it, first the younger moves.

100.

They would wait there while the questions were asked, be given drinks, and there would be more, when finished with those. When the boys were brought in, they would be made comfortable. They would be dressed nicely when going into the court, brought in there, nice shirts gotten for them tucked deep down into pants, brown, buttoned all the way up, nice belts, nice shoes.

101.

He wants to put them in the car to take them away from this place, but you only had to look at them then. The older in particular with his clothes shows all traces. Until things got quieter, they would have to hide. Until they saw no police, until they knew nobody is looking, still. He wipes at arms, legs, hands, so there will be nothing. He would take them to his place, get them washed, cleaned up, in case he needs to take them somewhere, shirtfronts in the car dark clothes they were going to have to get out of soon, trailing. The boys go back to brushing their pants, shorts slick material on the older, then up against the seats, backs bent over slickened. The air smells sodden metallic, the ocher clay ground in, prints rubbed down sweating next to him there on the seat, the smell of salt even up from the back.

The friend tells the boys how he has to stop, before they go any further driving toward the sign marked what's coming up, passing truck not slowing, the beams of another car coming another way, bridge they're not going over but back towards an open field they would all get out in, in a minute, the next place seen, somewhere no one is around. Not until there is a place quiet, deserted, would they stop for the boys to take off those clothes, parked out in the dark a ways from where no more motors come down so frequently. He would get them to where the new state's line starts, but clothes he can still smell. He's thinking he can put them in the trunk, and that was when he told them both to also get up in there. He couldn't be stopped with them. Just until he could make sure everything is cleared. He would drive back another way, not the same. There is enough space to breathe until then, legs and arms pressed smelling sharper, deeper, clothes salted, the sound sped.

102.

They would be hiding in a hole he has made, in their minds running still down into there where they would go, because it is not safe for them to come back out. He would tell them when it was right again, the friend who knows he has to watch out for himself. This time in the end a whole life taken.

Here years, years to be accepted. With a judge high up above a scale is set, precedent established. When considering character, reports must be taken into account, along with everything else. When they were free, once it was safe to drive around again with them, they'd go wherever. Other days other lights. That night, watch all the TV they wanted. He'd take them back inside but just until morning. He'd take them the next morning or the one after that, soon, in a matter of days.

103.

Each to live with their own degree of complicity, the friend, the oldest, serves longest, older brother eight years set and the youngest one less in a center.

104.

It does not that night in the living room get too far along there, the lazy chair and everything in it to be consumed, soaked through by authorities, and seen once they get the smoke more cleared, house opened back up. Nothing yet too all badly burnt. They keep it from reaching any closer, the body just a little bit propped still in the middle of the room in the chair, head all destroyed, and there to be examined, male, still completely dressed.

He had apparently not gotten off to bed yet, before it started, boots still on. A body that was smooth and has been glistening undergoing its trauma, mind only mildly intoxicated under the beer or two inside with dinner, hair graying at and around grazed bone, torn scalp.

In skin, he is said to look about forty, the base of the skull fractured, brain hemorrhaged, and pituitary gland lacerated. On cheeks and chin, several days' beard growth now over a split lip washed, in mustache, tissue and ashen skin. Red flecked back of the chair greased down and worn, there on the wall behind, knowing where to look a purpled gray seen matter and brain. They would have to get the body for photographs out of clothes. Woods jacket with long sleeves, green-brown pattern opened and removed, t-shirt underneath spotted, shown through around a goat saying. Next taken down are jeans and briefs, he was turned over, the long foreskin recorded in passing over the body, lower legs, feet "dirty" written inspection notes continue, calloused to a hardened extreme the hands.

Someone would eventually take it all away. Once there lived a man it was not so hard to believe this happening to really, eventually, if you've been ever anywhere close to what they were not going to anymore be living like, and the headlines wrapped all around, the headlines continuing, I imagine everyone has had the thought, if not every day at some point: how simple it would be to change everything just by doing the one thing. Picture your own father here, could you, as I did a man believing himself good as mine.

Born in Virginia and raised in Georgia, **DOUGLAS A. MARTIN** moved to New York at 25 and now resides in Brooklyn. Douglas's writing spans fiction and nonfiction, traversing poetry and prose with works translated into Italian, Japanese, and Portuguese. Past books include: *Once You Go Back* (Lambda Award nomination in the Gay Memoir/Biography category), *Branwell* (Ferro-Grumley Award finalist), several volumes of poetry, and a book of stories. *Outline of My Lover* was named an International Book of the Year in The Times Literary Supplement and adapted in part by the Forsythe Company for their ballet and live film "Kammer/Kammer." In addition to the twentieth anniversary edition of *Outline of My Lover*, publications with Nightboat Books include a book-length essay and lyric study, *Acker*, and a triptych of of novellas, *Your Body Figured*.

NIGHTBOAT BOOKS

Nightboat Books, a nonprofit organization, seeks to develop audiences for writers whose work resists convention and transcends boundaries. We publish books rich with poignancy, intelligence, and risk. Please visit nightboat.org to learn about our titles and how you can support our future publications.

The following individuals have supported the publication of this book. We thank them for their generosity and commitment to the mission of Nightboat Books:

Kazim Ali

Anonymous

Jean C. Ballantyne

Photios Giovanis

Amanda Greenberger

Anne Marie Macari

Elizabeth Motika

Benjamin Taylor

Jerrie Whitfield & Richard Motika

In addition, this book has been made possible, in part, by grants from the National Endowment for the Arts, the New York City Department of Cultural Affairs in partnership with the City Council, and the New York State Council on the Arts Literature Program.